shell game

sarah r. shaber

shell game

Thomas Dunne Books

St. Martin's Minotaur

New York

This is a work of fiction. All of the characters, organizations, and events portrayed in this novel are either products of the author's imagination or are used fictitiously.

THOMAS DUNNE BOOKS.
An imprint of St. Martin's Press.

www.thomasdunnebooks.com
www.stmartins.com

Library of Congress Cataloging-in-Publication Data

Shaber, Sarah R.
Shell game / Sarah R. Shaber.—1st ed.
p. cm.
ISBN-13: 978-0-312-35602-6
ISBN-10: 0-312-35602-1
1. Shaw, Simon (Fictitious character)—Fiction. 2. History teachers—Fiction. 3. College teachers—Fiction. 4. Archaeology— Fiction. 5. North Carolina—Fiction. I. Title.

PS3569.H226 S53 2007
813'.54—dc22

2006050615

First Edition: March 2007

10 9 8 7 6 5 4 3 2 1

*For my dear son, Sam, the other artist in the family,
who grew up watching me scribble*

acknowledgments

I seem to have an obsession with Oakwood Cemetery, a lovely, historic graveyard in old Raleigh. I set a scene there in every one of the Simon Shaw novels that take place in Simon's hometown. As always, Joe Freed, manager of Oakwood Cemetery, cheerfully answered all my questions, no matter how peculiar they seemed.

Thanks to Dr. Bill Oliver, director of the North Carolina Archaeological Research Office, and Gregory Richardson, executive director of the North Carolina Commission of Indian Affairs, for assisting me with my research. Any errors in this book are mine, not theirs.

And thank you, Amy Jo Barr, for all your help.

author's note

In this book I use the newer abbreviation "BP," which means "Before Present," instead of the older form, "BC," when describing prehistoric age. Pottery once dated to 1200 BC is now dated to 3200 BP. In converting dates from "BC," "BCE" (Before Common Era), and "Before Contact" (before 1492) to "BP," I might have made a mistake or two. If so, I apologize in advance. Math is not my strong suit.

Theories about the colonization of the Americas abound. I've mentioned the most prevalent views in this book, but I make no guarantees that I covered them all, or that some future discovery won't change everything!

During my background reading and interviewing for this book I observed that the term "Indian" was used more often than "Native American," even among the Indians I talked with, so I have used "Indian" more often in the text.

From the *Raleigh News & Observer*, July 17, 2001

PREHISTORIC SITE YIELDS HUMAN REMAINS

BADIN, NORTH CAROLINA—Archaeologists at work not far from Hardaway, a famous prehistoric site in Stanly County, announced today that they have found the first human remains ever unearthed here in association with a pre-Clovis spearhead and an early hearth. The remains were found near Narrows Dam on Badin Lake, opposite the peninsula where Hardaway is located, in the Uwharrie National Forest. This find, according to Dr. Lawrence Mabry, professor of southern prehistory at the University of North Carolina at Chapel Hill, places North Carolina squarely into the contentious discussion over the origins of the earliest inhabitants of the Americas. The bones were found by graduate student Martha Dunn, a member of Dr. Mabry's team excavating the new site. Using radiocarbon dating, the hearth has been dated to approximately 12,000 BC, or, as paleontologists prefer, 14,000 BP (Before Present).

shell game

1

I'm not afraid of dying. I just don't want to be there when it happens.

—WOODY ALLEN

SIMON KNEW INSTANTLY THAT SOMEONE HE CARED ABOUT was dead. Walker Jones, the chairman of his department, and Sophie Berelman, another colleague, hovered in the hall corridor outside the lecture hall, waiting for his class to end. Sophie leaned against the oak-wainscoted wall, gazing fixedly at the floor, repeatedly glancing at her watch, looking miserable, while Walker, inured by years of experience coping with the troubles of his colleagues, just waited stoically, arms crossed. Vultures perched on the staircase banister outside the room would have been less conspicuous.

Seconds before the bell rang, Simon's students began to shuffle their papers and water bottles into their back-packs. They emptied the old-fashioned stadium seating in no time, leaving Simon alone in the echoing lecture room. For once no one lingered behind to talk to him.

Simon turned and started erasing his scribbles from

the whiteboard, the only modern fixture in the room, dreading the next few minutes. He mentally reviewed the various ages and infirmities of his aunts and uncles, and braced himself for the bad news. After the last student had left, Walker and Sophie came in. Sophie closed the door behind them.

"Bad news," Simon said matter-of-factly.

" 'Fraid so," Walker said. Sophie laid a hand on Simon's shoulder. "David Morgan died this morning," Walker said. Walker pulled a chair out from behind a desk while Sophie guided Simon into it.

Simon wasn't prepared for this, not that anyone is ever prepared to learn about an unexpected death. His friend David Morgan was forty-two years old. He didn't take any worse care of himself than most people Simon knew. He must have had an accident of some kind.

"I just saw him a couple of days ago," Simon said, as if that meant anything.

"I'm so sorry," Sophie said again.

"Car wreck?" Simon asked.

"No," Walker said.

"What, then?" Simon asked.

The two glanced at each other, hesitating.

"He's got to know," Sophie said to Walker. She turned to Simon. "He was murdered."

SIMON FOUND HIMSELF SITTING on the worn leather sofa in Walker's office, his hands wrapped around a steaming mug of coffee. Walker poured a shot of Jack Daniel's into the mug. Simon drank half of it in one gulp.

Walker sat down next to him.

"We've canceled your classes for a couple of days, of course," he said. "Marcus will be here in a few minutes to drive you home."

Simon finished his coffee without speaking, collecting his thoughts and emotions.

"I want to know what happened," he said. He tried to remember Morgan's schedule. Had he gone to the office today? Was he out on a dig?

"We don't know yet," Walker said. "A package delivery-man found the body this morning. The police are still at the house."

Simon's friend Marcus Clegg arrived, carrying his briefcase and Simon's, too.

"Hey," he said, touching Simon briefly on his arm. "I am so damn sorry. Let's go to your place." He raised Simon's briefcase. "I think I've got all your stuff. I'll wait with you, until . . . ."

"Until what?" Simon said. "Until Morgan's not dead anymore?"

"Until we know more," Sophie said, placating him.

"I don't need a babysitter," Simon said.

"You shouldn't be alone for a few days," Marcus said.

"Stop being so goddamned nice to me."

"Live with it," Walker said. "We're all going to be nice as hell to you, whether you like it or not. Now go home."

Once in Marcus's car, Simon's fury overtook him. With both fists he slammed the dash of Marcus's restored 1967 Carolina blue Mustang, his pride and joy. Marcus winced but didn't say anything.

"Take me to Morgan's house," Simon said, speaking with a clenched jaw to keep his voice from wavering.

Marcus shook his head. "Not a good idea," he said.

"I need to know what happened."

"I know this is hard, but I think—"

"I don't care what you think. Either take me to Morgan's house or let me out of the car, I'll walk there."

Silently Marcus turned toward Morgan's neighborhood.

"I'm sorry," Simon said. "I shouldn't have spoken to you like that."

"Under the circumstances you're entitled to behave as badly as you like, for a while, anyway," Marcus said.

They stopped in front of David Morgan's modest ranch home, or rather, they stopped a half block away because an ambulance, a City County Bureau of Investigation crime van, and a couple of police cars were parked in front of the house. Bystanders lined the boundary of the yellow scene-of-crime tape and gawked, whispering among themselves.

Simon snapped. He got out of the car and took off at a run down the street. His path was blocked by a burly policeman. Simon was a small man, and the policeman almost lifted him off the ground while restraining him.

"I need to go inside," Simon said. "I want to see him."

"The victim was a close friend of his," Marcus said to the policeman, catching up to them. He gripped Simon's free arm, and both men kept a tight hold on him.

"Sorry," the policeman said. "This is a crime scene. No one allowed in until the investigators are finished with their work."

"I know Sergeant Gates from the homicide division," Simon said. "Call him, he'll vouch for me."

"The victim's corpse is already loaded into the ambulance."

As if to frustrate Simon even further, the ambulance's engine fired, and the vehicle pulled away from the curb.

"There's nothing you can do here," Marcus said.

"We can do our jobs better if civilians don't interfere with our investigations," the policeman said.

"Stop patronizing me, both of you. I'm not leaving. I insist on knowing everything that happened here."

"We haven't come to any conclusions yet, Simon." Detective-Sergeant Otis Gates's voice boomed from a body that matched it, an ex-footballer's husky frame. He'd come out of the house behind them.

"Otis, thank God," Simon said. Marcus and the policeman released Simon's arms, and the policeman, catching a nod from Otis, went back to his post.

Otis Gates was dressed, impeccably as usual, in a brown pin-striped suit. Gates was a big African-American man, a devout Baptist, and a native North Carolinian with a law-and-order perspective on life. He and Simon Shaw, a liberal academic whose Jewish mother had moved south from Queens and married into an old Boone family, had become improbable friends over the past few years, after Otis had recruited Simon, a professor of history at nearby Kenan College, to help him solve a murder committed in 1926.

At the time Simon accepted Otis's request mostly to distract himself from his divorce, and had surprised himself by becoming intensely involved in the case. He quickly realized that professional historians were natural detectives. Like skilled homicide investigators, they asked intrusive questions, mobilized any resources needed to answer them, and drew conclusions based on evidence. Without any scruples they probed deeply into family history, possible motives, and character. Simon solved that 1926 murder, and since then had cracked several more very cold cases. He'd become somewhat famous, dubbed a "forensic historian" by the press, attracting some celebrity, and, it must be said, a bit of criticism, even jealousy, from a few of his colleagues. It didn't help that Kenan College, a small liberal arts school situated on a lovely campus in downtown Raleigh, publicized Simon's cases for their public relations value for the college.

This murder was different, though, this was immediate and personal, and Simon responded to it the way any normal person would, with shock, anger, and grief. So despite their friendship Otis dealt with him professionally, with firmness as well as compassion.

"You can't go inside, Simon," Gates said. "There's nothing productive you can do here, except stay out of our way."

"Tell me what happened."

"Dr. Morgan died from a heavy blow to the head, from behind. He was sitting at his desk, working, I suppose, because his laptop was on. Dr. Morgan didn't know what hit him, if that's any comfort. The paramedic said he died instantly. Other than that I can't tell you anything else, not right now."

"But why would someone murder him?"

"I have no idea. It's early days yet."

"He has a sister in Tennessee."

"Notified. She's on her way."

Simon, despite his scholarly vocation, was a man of action. Otis realized he needed something to do.

"His dogs are at the vet's," Gates said. "They were

found unconscious in the backyard. Why don't you check on them?"

Morgan's dogs were like his children.

"I'll drive you there," Marcus said, seizing on an opportunity to get Simon away.

"We'll be here most of the night working the crime scene," Gates said. "I'll come by in the morning and tell you what I can."

"I was his closest friend," Simon said. "Shouldn't you question me?"

"In the morning," Gates said. "You go on, now."

THE YOUNG VETERINARIAN IN the crisp white coat knew the whole story. She treated Simon very kindly, which irritated him. He didn't want to be treated kindly. He wanted to put his fist through the glass of the office door and explode with misplaced anger, but he managed to check himself and be civil.

"The dogs are in the back," she said. "Want to see them?"

"Please," Simon said.

MORGAN'S BLACK LABRADOR RETRIEVERS lay, prone and unconscious, in individual cages. Intravenous bottles hung over them, clear tubes snaking into big soft paws wrapped with tape. Both were monitored. The machines beeped as the peaks and valleys of their vital signs moved across black screens.

Rex, the oldest dog at ten, looked the worst. Simon

couldn't tell that he was even breathing, although weak respirations showed on the monitor. Simon reached through the bars of the cage and stroked Rex's white-flecked muzzle, but got no response.

Luke, the three-year old, looked better. His eyelids opened a crack and his tail moved when Simon touched a paw.

"Are they going to live?" Simon asked.

"I think Luke will," the vet said. "I don't know about Rex. He's older, already had some heart disease."

"My friend would want them to have the best care possible," Simon said. "I'll take care of the bills."

"We're doing everything your doctor would do for you if you overdosed," she said. "We just have to wait and see."

"So they were drugged."

"Yeah," she said. "We've drawn blood samples for the police."

At the front desk Simon signed the papers that would commit him to the dogs' bills, and left all his phone numbers.

"We'll call you if there's any change," the vet said. "And I am so sorry. We all liked Dr. Morgan very much."

"Thanks," Simon said.

"You realize what this means," Simon said, climbing back into Marcus's car. "Morgan's death was planned. His murderer drugged the dogs so they couldn't sound an alarm."

"I know," Marcus said. "Sergeant Gates told me, when he called the history department this morning, that it looked premeditated."

"But in God's name, why?"

"I can't imagine," Marcus said.

David Morgan was an archaeologist for the state of North Carolina. He was the most uncomplicated man Simon knew. Never married, he was absorbed in his work, the prehistory of North Carolina. Crisscrossing the state in his black Ford pickup, dogs riding in back in the camper, surveying and excavating, was his life. His staff had to nudge him to get a haircut when he needed one. Even in his office he wore work boots, jeans, and flannel shirts. Simon had never seen him in a tie. Morgan's idea of a party was two beers and a UNC basketball game on television. He had few relationships—his sister and her family, Simon, a couple of old friends from graduate school, a woman Episcopal priest in Durham he insisted he wasn't dating. Then Simon remembered.

"Have you told Trina?" he asked Marcus.

"Not yet," Marcus said.

Trina was Marcus's brilliant thirteen-year-old daughter, the second of his four girls. She had met Morgan a few years ago when Simon and Morgan joined the Cleggs at their beach house on Thanksgiving, and instantly bonded with him. After a weekend of trailing him and his metal detector up and down the beach, she decided to become an archaeologist herself. Morgan, who until he met Trina claimed to dislike children, had been both bemused and flattered, giving her tours of his dig sites and letting her visit his lab.

ONCE IN HIS OWN home and out of public view, Simon succumbed to shock. He dropped onto his sofa and put his head in his hands. He tried to absorb the fact of David Morgan's death, his murder. Marcus sat down next to him, but seemed to know not to try to comfort him.

"I hope it's true," Simon said.

"What?"

"That he didn't know what hit him," Simon said.

He wondered why he thought that ignorance of impending death was positive. Because he didn't want his friend to be afraid? What about making peace and all that? What would he, Simon, want in the same circumstances? He couldn't say.

He needed a stiff drink.

"Look," Marcus said. "I can't stay, I wish I could, but I've got to get home. I need to talk to Trina before news of the murder gets out."

"How do you think she'll take it?"

"I haven't a clue. She's thirteen. Her behavior is unpredictable under the best of circumstances these days."

"I'll be fine," Simon said, wondering how much bourbon was in his liquor cabinet.

AFTER MARCUS LEFT, SIMON made a beeline for his liquor cupboard. He poured a good two fingers of Maker's Mark into a glass to calm his nerves, filled it with Coke to settle his stomach, and stirred in two preventative doses of Goody's headache powders. He took the glass out onto his porch, where he sat and sipped and listened to the construction noises from a new library being built two blocks away.

Simon wasn't one of those who bemoaned the city's growth. He liked Raleigh's down-home upscale feel, the coffee shops next to the barbecue joints, the county speedway coexisting with a new Saks, lofts and condos infilling the empty lots scattered in old Victorian neighborhoods, opera at the new concert hall competing with country music at the state fair. You could buy a fresh bagel or a Krispy Kreme doughnut for breakfast, depending on your mood. And Raleigh was still just two hours from the beach and four hours from the mountains.

The construction noise ceased, the workday was over. Evening came earlier every day now. Handfuls of long brown needles drifted down from the loblolly pine in his backyard, blanketing the ground below. Squirrels roamed the tall tree's branches, breaking away to rob his neighbor's restocked bird feeder. A graceful maple, tipped with scarlet but still thick with green foliage on its lower branches, stood poised between summer and autumn. Simon inhaled the cozy odor of smoke from evening fires wafting around the neighborhood. In a matter of days dioramas constructed from straw bales, pumpkins, and gourds would replace the jungle of potted plants on his neighbors' front stoops.

It would be a long night, the first of many, he knew. He'd experienced grief before, when his parents had died, and he had a good idea what to expect. All the psychological stages had to be endured before balance could come back into his life. It couldn't be avoided. Best to get it over with.

He went back inside for more bourbon. He would send away whatever poor soul had been drafted to stay with him tonight. Then he could get drunk in peace.

THERE WAS A TIME when seeing Julia McGloughlin standing on his front step with a suitcase would have made his heart shudder with anticipation. That was until they'd broken up for the second time, and before Morgan's murder and four ounces of bourbon had muffled his feelings.

"Drunk already?" Julia said.

"What are you doing here?" Simon asked.

"Staying with you for a few days," Julia said, coming inside and dropping her suitcase on the floor.

"You don't need to," Simon said. "I'll be fine. Honestly."

"How much have you had to drink?" Julia said. "Have you had any dinner?"

"Who cares, and no, I'm not hungry."

"You need soup," she said, picking up the grocery bag and heading into the kitchen.

He followed her.

"Homemade?" he asked.

"Are you kidding?" she said. "Fresh Market special. Potato."

She knew where his pots and pans were. After she dumped the soup into a saucepan and set it to low, she came over and put her arms around him. He allowed himself to lean against her for a second.

"I am so sorry," she said. Thank goodness she didn't say anything else. Simon was finding he had a low threshold for platitudes.

"Thanks," Simon said. "I just can't believe it."

"Neither can I."

She smelled of Giorgio, just like always, but it did nothing for him. Nor did the proximity of her body tempt him. A carapace of grief and anger encased him, blocking all other emotions.

"Force some food down," Julia said. "You need to soak up that booze."

He managed a few spoonfuls of soup and a couple of crackers. Then he refreshed his bourbon. Julia didn't try to stop him. She washed their bowls and glasses.

"Do you want me to leave you alone?" she asked.

"Please."

"I'll be upstairs reading if you need me," she said. "I know my way to the guest room."

SIMON WOKE UP THE next morning on his sofa with the worst hangover of his life. His head throbbed and his stomach surged with nausea. The morning light streaming through the living room windows drove spikes of pain deep into his brain.

Julia sat opposite him, in his father's old leather Mission armchair, reading the morning newspaper. She'd pulled her long auburn hair back in a ponytail, and wore flannel pajama pants and a sweatshirt. As usual when they weren't dating, she'd gotten too thin.

"Did you do enough damage?" she asked.

"For now," he said. He groped his way into the kitchen, got a cold Coke out of the refrigerator, stirred a couple of Goody's powders into it, and raided the small stash of codeine he kept for special occasions. He took three pills, filled an ice bag, and got into the tiny shower in his downstairs bathroom. With the ice pack pressed tight to his head, and hot water pouring down on him, he shed the first and last tears he would over David Morgan's death.

Fifteen minutes later Julia knocked on the bathroom door.

"You okay?" she asked.

"Yeah," Simon said.

"Need anything?"

"Not unless you can keep the hot water from running out."

"I'm going to fix some eggs. Don't suppose you want any."

"No, thanks."

When the water turned chilly Simon cut off the shower. He wrapped a towel around himself and went into the kitchen. Julia had seen him in less than a towel many times, and frankly, he didn't care.

"I'm going to go upstairs and get dressed."

"Okay," she said. "Otis called. He'll be here in half an hour. I made some toast for you. You should try to eat it."

Upstairs Simon shaved and put on clean jeans, a worn black Kenan College sweatshirt, and athletic shoes. The codeine had masked the worst of his headache. He had a feeling he would be seeking out numbness in any form he could for a while.

Back downstairs he tore a slice of buttered toast into pieces and forced himself to eat it. Julia left him alone, drinking more coffee in the living room. Simon's three cats, who were used to far more attention from him than they were getting, vainly tried to distract him, rubbing along his legs and meowing pitifully. After a minute or two they gave up and went through the pet door outside.

Simon put his head down on the kitchen table.

"Julia," he called, his voice muffled.

"Yeah."

"Thanks for being here."

She came into the kitchen, leaned over him, and hugged him tightly, and he grasped her hands and held on.

"I'll stay as long as you need me," she said.

"Just don't try to comfort me."

"I won't, I promise."

She released him, and he got another Coke from the refrigerator. His stomach began to settle down.

"When I was a kid," he said, "I always thought the world would make sense to me someday. I was wrong."

"I know what you mean. After working for the police department, I've decided there's no point in wasting energy wondering why life is the way it is. All you can do is cope with it as best you can."

Julia was an attorney who worked as the Raleigh Police Department's legal counsel. Simon had met her on his first case with Otis. They had dated intensely for a while until the affair fizzled out. Neither of them seemed to get what they needed from the relationship. Julia just couldn't commit to a future with Simon, for reasons she could never explain adequately. Simon suspected that his height and family background bothered her more than she would admit. And he wasn't ambitious. He'd never leave Kenan. He loved teaching undergraduates, and that's what he intended to do for the rest of his life.

Despite a popular culture that glorified the single life, like most men Simon wanted a happy monogamous relationship, complete with mortgage, kids, and minivan. For him casual sex was an acceptable stopgap measure, not a way of life. His first marriage had failed, but he was eager to try again.

Otis Gates let himself into Simon's house after rapping on the door once. Simon could tell by his body language that he'd come on business. He'd proceed as a detective-sergeant of homicide first, and a friend second.

Julia made no move to excuse herself. As the attorney for the police department, she would know all the facts of the case eventually, anyway.

"You could look worse," Gates said to Simon.

"I'm making every effort to get there."

"Coffee, Otis?" Julia asked.

"Please," he said.

"Don't grin at me like that," she said. "And if you tell anyone at work I fetched you coffee, you'll regret it."

Otis took the Mission armchair and Simon sat on the couch. He was freezing. He leaned over and ignited the gas fire in his fireplace. By afternoon it would be warm enough to crank up the air-conditioning. Such was the weather in North Carolina, where you could experience all four seasons in a single week.

Otis removed a notebook and pencil from his inside pocket and licked the end of the pencil, a ritual Simon had observed many times.

"I have some questions for you," Gates said, "but if you like, I'll tell you what we know about Dr. Morgan's death first."

"Yes," Simon said, "please."

Julia brought in three mugs of coffee, set them down on the coffee table and took a seat on the sofa with Simon, her legs curled up beneath her.

"How much do you want to know?" Otis asked Simon.

"Everything you're comfortable telling me."

"Okay," Gates said. "The delivery guy brought a package to the house. He saw Dr. Morgan's truck in the driveway, so he figured he was at home. He knocked on the door, but there wasn't any answer. He got a funny feeling, because the dogs weren't barking, so he went around to the back door. He found the dogs out cold, and when he looked into the window of Dr. Morgan's office he saw him slumped over the desk. He called 911. When the paramedics and the police arrived, they discovered Morgan had been dead since early this morning."

"That's interesting," Simon said. "Morgan wasn't a morning person."

"So the neighbors said. Anyway, we secured the scene, transported the dogs to the vet, and questioned the neighbors. None of them saw or heard anything unusual."

"Did you find the murder weapon?"

"No, but we know it was a heavy, smooth, round object. The depression in Dr. Morgan's skull was quite deep. We searched every square inch of the neighborhood, looked in every trash can, under every bush. The murderer had enough smarts to dispose of it far from the murder scene. We may have a better description of the murder weapon after the autopsy. But I'm not expecting much help from the forensic evidence at the crime scene."

"What's the problem with the forensics?"

Otis sighed. "On television you see the crime scene investigators going over a scene and tweezing up just three items that turn out to be crucial to identifying the murderer. Do you realize how unlikely that is? Your friend Dr. Morgan wasn't very tidy. There were fingerprints from multiple individuals all over the house, several brands of empty beer bottles scattered around, the garbage cans were overflowing, the kitchen was a veritable museum of take-out containers, and the sink was full of dirty dishes. Who knows how many fingerprints there'll be on all that stuff, and you can't date it. It could be days old, or hours. And the hairs. It'll take weeks just to separate the dog hairs from the human hairs."

"I can tell you that the Sam Adams empties are mine," Simon said. "I was there watching a game a couple of nights ago. We had pizza."

"When will the autopsy be?" Julia asked.

"As soon as the medical examiner can arrange it," Gates said. "Dr. Morgan's sister is on her way from Tennessee to claim the body and arrange the funeral. Have you met her?" he asked Simon.

"No," Simon said. "Morgan always went to visit her, she never came here. Her husband is disabled and they have young kids. Has anyone called his girlfriend?"

"The Reverend Clare Monahan?" Gates said, consulting his notes. "She was his girlfriend?"

"Yeah," Simon said. "I think so. He claimed to dislike women, but that was a pose, I believe, until he found one that suited him. Has she been notified? If not, I'd like to call her myself."

"Already done, but she's out of the country. Her church says she's on a mission trip to Honduras, building a school out in the boonies. It'll take a few days to get a message to her, and then they don't know how long it will take her to get home."

"By that time there wouldn't be much point in her coming," Julia said. "The funeral will be over."

"When the forensic guys are finished with their analysis," Gates said, "I'd like you to walk through the house with me. See if you spot something important missing, out of place, anything at all."

"Of course," Simon said. "Are you thinking robbery?"

"Maybe. His wallet was missing."

"He carried a lot of cash, often several hundred dollars. He never learned to use an ATM."

"Any number of people might know that," Julia said. "I mean, he could open his wallet at the grocery store, or a restaurant, someone could see the cash, follow him home."

"Couldn't be that random, the dogs were drugged," Gates said.

"Then the murderer had to be a stranger," Simon said. "Those dogs would never bark at anyone they'd met before, even once."

"The stolen wallet could have been cover for a different crime," Gates said. "His laptop and a CD player weren't touched. You know the drill, we hear it often enough, most murders are personal, about sex, money, power."

"Morgan had no money and very little sex," Simon said.

"Can you think of any other reason why someone would want to murder him?"

"Are you joking? I can't imagine."

"Was he involved in anything controversial at work?"

"Whether or not some pot was late Woodland or early Mississippian, that's about it," Simon said.

"This is going to be a tough case. What we learned from our interviews jibes with everything you said. There are no obvious motives and, unless the autopsy tells us something we don't expect, little physical evidence that's useful. Are you sure Dr. Morgan wasn't involved in anything controversial?"

"Well . . ." Simon hesitated.

"What?"

"There's the Indian skeleton thing."

2

Leave the shower curtain on the inside of the tub.

—CONRAD N. HILTON, 1887–1979,
WHEN ASKED ON HIS DEATHBED IF HE HAD
ANY LAST WORDS OF WISDOM FOR THE WORLD

"WHAT SKELETON?" OTIS ASKED. "SHOULD I KNOW SOME-thing about this?"

"Uwharrie Man," Simon said. "He wouldn't be on your radar. He died about fourteen thousand years ago."

"This was an important part of Dr. Morgan's work?"

"Oh, yeah," Simon said. "Very. It's the earliest Paleo-Indian find in North Carolina. Some scholars think it adds legitimacy to the theory that early Americans arrived here on the continent many years earlier than we once thought."

"That's the controversial part?" Julia asked.

"There's more. The Lumbee Indian tribe wants the bones. They say that under the North Carolina law that protects human burials and human skeletal remains, Uwharrie Man should be turned over to them."

"What for?" Otis asked.

"Burial."

"You're kidding," Julia said.

"No, I'm not. The bones, and all the artifacts associated with it, are stored at the North Carolina Museum of Natural Sciences. There's been talk of endowing a dedicated laboratory devoted to its study. All that's on hold now."

"So what did Dr. Morgan have to do with this?" Otis asked.

"He was on a committee appointed by the governor to make the final decision disposing of the remains."

"Whether the museum or the Lumbee get the bones?" Julia asked.

"Yeah. It's been a difficult job, too. There have been meetings, and expert testimony, and pages of research. All the committee members were under a lot of pressure, as you can imagine."

"Who else was on this committee?" Otis asked, scribbling away in his notebook.

"Let's see," Simon said. "A representative of the Lumbee nation, the director of the Museum of Natural Sciences, the hotshot professor from Chapel Hill who found the bones in the first place, some others. You can get their names from Henry Klett, he's the executive director of the museum."

"Where did Dr. Morgan stand on this issue?"

"I don't think he'd made up his mind yet," Simon said.

"Surely he wouldn't be murdered over such a thing," Julia said.

"Academic rivalries can be vicious," Simon said. "I once saw a fistfight at the American Historical Association convention between two doctoral students who got into an argument during a panel discussion. Blood was shed, teeth were lost. I could ask around about the committee, if you like."

"I'll take care of it," Gates said to Simon. "You're to say out of this case."

Simon didn't respond.

"I mean it," Gates said. "You let the police handle this. Don't get involved. You were too close to Dr. Morgan."

"I appreciate the advice," Simon said. "But you can't expect me to sit here and do nothing."

"I expect exactly that."

"There'll be plenty for you to do," Julia said to Simon. "Dr. Morgan's sister will need help, there's the funeral—"

"Don't placate me."

"Then don't interfere," Gates said. "This is not one of your historical cold cases. This murder happened yesterday, and the murderer is still at large."

AFTER OTIS LEFT AND Julia went to work, Simon couldn't bear the quiet and inactivity. Of course he had no intention of investigating Morgan's murder. But he had to do something, anything, to pass the time, at least until the afternoon, when he would give himself permission to drink more bourbon. So he went in to his office at the history department, even though he didn't have class.

Since Marcus had driven him home yesterday, Simon had left his Thunderbird on campus. He walked the few blocks from his home to Kenan under a canopy of autumn color that ranged from scarlet through copper and orange to lemon yellow. Few leaves had dropped yet, but acorns, pecans, and spiky sweetgum husks littered the ground. The sounds of the Broughton High School marching band practicing a Sousa piece carried clearly through the crisp air. The day was so lovely it was painful, remembering as Simon did that his friend would never see another day like it.

"You shouldn't be here," Judy Smith, the departmental secretary, said to him.

"What should I be doing?" Simon asked. "The crossword puzzle?"

When he saw her hurt expression he apologized.

"It's okay," she said. "I understand."

Why is it, Simon wondered as he went down the hall to his office, that we can't tolerate sympathy when we need it the most?

Sitting at his father's old mahogany desk, surrounded by his own mementos and books and papers, didn't afford Simon the comfort he expected. He felt just as unhappy and restless as he had at home. He had no papers to grade, no lectures to prepare, and he'd be worthless to any student who might need his help.

A tentative knock at his door interrupted his brooding. He could hardly not answer it, since it was obvious that he was in his office.

"Come on in," he said, and instantly regretted it.

Maya Ott's perpetual submissive posture always irritated him, but he figured it must have worked for her in high school, or she wouldn't still be using it.

"I'm real sorry to hear about your friend, Dr. Shaw," Maya said.

"Thanks, Maya. Sit down, what can I do for you?"

Maya sat, dropping her book bag on the floor with a

thud. She tossed her straight brown hair behind her shoulders and slumped into the chair.

"You gave me an F on my last paper," she said. "It's not fair. It was a really, really good paper."

"Maya, did you even bother to read my comments? You plagiarized! Most of that paper wasn't your work."

"I didn't, I swear!"

"You used several phrases that didn't seem like your usual style," Simon said, "and I use the word 'style' loosely. So I googled those phrases, and guess what? Your essay contained complete sentences and paragraphs pulled from an article published in the *North Carolina Historical Review* a couple of years ago. That's plagiarism, pure and simple."

Maya seemed so surprised that Simon could almost believe she didn't know what he was talking about.

"Kenan's honor code allows you to make one mistake," Simon said. "Another one and you're out."

Maya pouted, and Simon felt his patience, always limited on such occasions, ebbing away.

"But, Dr. Shaw," she said, "it's not what you think. My brother wrote that paper at State last year, so he's the one who plagiarized, not me! I had no idea!"

"Whether you got it from your brother or a little yellow bird, it's not your work. It's cheating."

"Tell you what, my brother got an A on that paper. How about you give me a C-minus, and I swear I won't do it again."

Maya must not have liked the look on his face, because she immediately got up and left without saying another word.

Simon often wondered if his students cheated occasionally just to test him. Like teenagers challenging their parents, they wanted to see if he gave enough of a damn to catch them. Simon did. He often took a stack of term papers and his laptop to Helios, a neighborhood coffeehouse, to spend an afternoon drinking coffee, eating scones, and googling suspect phrases. Most of Simon's students were honest kids who worked hard at their studies. But a sizable minority had a murky notion of literary honesty. They seemed to believe that it was okay to plagiarize if they were pressed for time, that their tuition bought them a minimum grade, and that the sole point of graduating from college was to acquire the right job.

Simon had an old-fashioned view of a college education. Working was inevitable. Jobs happened when the rent was due. But college was a once-in-a-lifetime opportunity to get an education that would sustain you your entire life. Simon had taught history majors who had become bankers and doctors, and he figured they were better at their jobs because of it.

To distract himself Simon turned on his computer and checked Kenan's Web site for news and announcements, then realized that the link from his biography to an old *People* magazine profile of him was still active. He'd lost count of how often he'd asked that it be deleted. He forced himself to count to ten, then twenty, before he called the college's public relations office. He left a brief, explicit message for the director, Rufus King, to remove the link immediately, threatening to call the president of the college if he ignored Simon's wishes again.

It wasn't that the article wasn't favorable, or that he hadn't gotten a bit of a kick out of it himself, but that Simon dreaded morphing into a celebrity professor. He'd seen it happen to others. First came the bestselling book, then the television appearances, then the addiction to honorariums and autographing sessions. The celebrity professor became too busy to teach more than one "graduate seminar" a year, then finally made the inevitable mistakes caused by cutting and pasting the work of research assistants in the push to publish a book a year.

Simon was a historian and teacher first and foremost, and his academic credibility was important to him. He wrote about his cases only for the *North Carolina Historical Review*. He'd succumbed to the *People* interview in a moment of conceit, relished the attention, and now was paying a steep price, becoming public relations fodder for the college.

Without thinking consciously about what he was doing, Simon picked up a stapler, took aim, and flung it across the room. It narrowly missed his framed Pulitzer Prize certificate hanging on the opposite wall, then ricocheted off a metal trash can with a mighty crash.

Marcus Clegg cracked open Simon's office door and poked his head inside.

"Break anything?" he asked.

"Unfortunately, no."

Marcus came in, picked the stapler up off the floor, and handed it to Simon.

"Here," he said, "try again."

Sophie came in behind him.

"What are we doing?" she asked. "Throwing stuff? Can I help?"

"I doubt the three of us together could do enough damage to satisfy me," Simon said. "What were you doing hovering outside my door?"

"Getting up the nerve to speak to you," Sophie said. "How are you coping?"

"Not very well," Simon said. "You guys were right, I need to stay away from here and go home, where pitching fits won't imperil my career."

Sophie and Marcus took the chairs in front of Simon's desk. Sophie nicely filled out her blue jeans, which Simon appreciated even if she was happily married and unavailable, and as always pulled her thick dark hair back from her face with twin barrettes. Black-rimmed cat's-eye glasses gave her an air of scholarly hipness. She'd returned to work in the fall semester after having a baby girl. Simon was glad to see that motherhood had curbed her workaholism. She specialized in Holocaust oral history, and chafed over the knowledge that many survivors would die before she had a chance to interview them.

Marcus and his wife, Marianne, were among Simon's closest friends. They were grown-up flower children who lived outside of Raleigh. Marcus wore his brown hair down to his shoulders, while Marianne grew organic vegetables, baked bread, and raised their four daughters. When Simon first met them he wondered if their lifestyle was a pose, but over the years he'd learned differently. Even the acclaim given Marcus's first book, *The Recantation of Galileo*, hadn't spoiled them. Marcus still brought his lunch to work in a brown bag, and Marianne kept her part-time job editing manuscripts at home for the Oxford University Press.

"I'm losing my mind, frankly," Simon said. "I can't stop thinking about Morgan's death. I obviously shouldn't be here, but there's nothing at home to keep me busy."

"Do the police have any leads?" Marcus asked.

"None they're sharing with me," Simon said.

"I didn't know Dr. Morgan well, just through you, Simon, but I can't imagine why anyone would want to kill him," Sophie said.

"I've been obsessing about that," Simon said. "The only part of Morgan's life that was at all controversial was his membership on the committee to deal with Uwharrie Man. By the way, I haven't seen Jack. Is he here today? I want to talk to him."

Jack Kingfisher was a new assistant professor specializing in southern history. He was also a Cherokee Indian.

"Not for the rest of the week," Sophie said. "He's at a symposium in Connecticut."

"Don't take offense, Simon," Marcus said, "but who knows what was going on in Morgan's life? He could have been, I don't know, making methamphetamine in the basement. I'm exaggerating, of course, but you know what I mean."

"Or, couldn't his death have been unintentional?" Sophie asked.

"The dogs were sedated," Simon said. "That makes it look premeditated."

"But maybe the killer didn't intend to murder Dr. Morgan—maybe he was after something else," Marcus said. "Other than the few hundred bucks in his wallet, I mean."

"Like what? His complete collection of Stephen King paperbacks?" Simon asked. "He didn't own anything valuable."

"Are you sure?" Sophie asked. "Doesn't that depend on your definition of 'valuable'?"

"One thing Otis told me was peculiar," Simon said. "Morgan died working at his desk early in the morning.

But he wasn't a morning person. He needed two alarm clocks and a full pot of coffee to get anywhere by nine."

"So maybe the killer drugged the dogs to keep them from waking Morgan up, broke into the house, and then had to kill him after finding him awake," Morgan said.

"If that's the case, we still don't know what the guy wanted that was worth the effort. Much less who it was."

FOR THE FIRST TIME since he bought his 2000 black Thunderbird, Simon took no joy in driving it. He could have been in a used station wagon for all he cared. He drove slowly toward his home. It wasn't even time for lunch, and he felt like it was midnight. He rehashed his conversations with Otis and Marcus and Sophie. Maybe because he was a historian and an academic, he kept returning to Morgan's work with Uwharrie Man.

When he got home Simon called the Museum of Natural Sciences and spoke to the director's assistant.

"You're not the first person to call this morning," she said in an excited voice. "The police just spoke to Dr. Klett."

"I'd like to talk to him, too," Simon said. "If possible I'd like to get the names of the persons on the committee David Morgan—"

"Dr. Klett's not in the office right now," she said. "He's gone into a meeting with the museum's Board of Trustees. But I can give you those names myself. It's public information."

SIMON HUNG UP THE phone and went over the brief list Klett's assistant had given him. The committee members were Lawrence Mabry, the professor from UNC–Chapel Hill who supervised the dig where Uwharrie Man had been found; Henry Klett, director of the museum where the skeleton was stored; Brad Lowery, a pharmacist, member of the Lumbee Tribal Council, and unsuccessful candidate for Congress; and Brenda Lambert, head of the North Carolina Commission of Indian Affairs. David Morgan represented the Office of State Archaeology. Five members, five votes. Simon had met Klett, but didn't know the others. He remembered reading a couple of newspaper articles when Mabry discovered Uwharrie Man, and he'd watched Lowery on a televised debate during the last election season. Lowery was thirty or so, stocky, underdressed for the occasion, a fluent if indignant speaker. Looking at the short roster, he couldn't help but see Morgan as the tie-breaker. Surely Klett and Mabry would favor the study of the skeleton, and Lowery and Lambert would want it returned to the Lumbee. Just how vested were these individuals in what happened to Uwharrie Man?

Simon massaged his temples, hard. Then he rummaged for a notebook and a pen. He always thought better with his tools in his hands.

He rehashed his conversation with Marcus and Sophie. Could the murder have been accidental, the result of a botched robbery attempt? It couldn't have been random, because the perpetrator knew Morgan had dogs and slept late. Would someone go to the extremes of drugging the dogs and breaking into the house for a few hundred dollars? If not, what else did Morgan have that was valuable? Simon thought of Morgan's home office, obsessively organized compared to the rest of his life, stacked with

files, books, mementos, boxes of index cards, journals, sou-
venirs, and clippings. Was any of it valuable, and to
whom?

If Morgan's murder wasn't the result of a burglary
gone bad, what could have been the murderer's motive?
Simon was as sure that Morgan would never do anything
illegal as he was sure of his own name, but he'd assume for
now it was possible. What illegal activity was feasible? It
had to involve something valuable enough to provoke vio-
lence. Native American artifacts were the center of a wide-
spread black market. It was beyond credulity that Morgan
was stealing pots and spearheads himself, but could he
have caught someone at it? Possibly.

Then there was Simon's own suspicion. Morgan was a
voting member of the committee to dispose of Uwharrie
Man, charged with deciding whether to allow an extraor-
dinary find to be studied by archaeologists and anthropologists, or to deliver it to the Lumbee for reburial. To
the average person this might not seem like an important
controversy, but Simon knew the stakes were huge for the
people involved.

He'd talked with Morgan a few times about the committee, and, although Morgan had never indicated how he
intended to vote, they'd gone over some of the problems
involved. The ethical issues were serious enough—how to
treat human remains, who owns ancient artifacts, what is a
legitimate archaeological site and what isn't. Many Native
Americans believed that scientists had been digging up
their graveyards and disturbing their dead for years. For the
anthropologists and archaeologists, their careers depended
on being able to excavate and study their finds.

Simon controlled an impulse to try to locate Jack Kingfisher at his symposium and pester him for information on what the Native American community thought about their own archaeological sites.

He knew Otis Gates and his team of homicide detectives and forensic examiners would expertly analyze all the forensic evidence surrounding Morgan's murder, exhaustively interview his coworkers and neighbors and friends, decipher his computer files, and map out his recent movements. Simon wasn't at all sure how well they could evaluate the professional issues involved. He would do that for them.

Simon felt infinitely better. This was something he could do for his dead friend, and keeping busy would help him cope.

The phone rang three times before he registered it and picked up the receiver.

"I'm Denise McGrath," the woman's voice on the other end of the line said, "David Morgan's sister."

"Of course," Simon said. "Where are you?"

"At his house."

"I wish you'd called me sooner," Simon said. "I could have picked you up at the airport. What can I do to help?"

"Didn't he tell you?" she asked.

"Tell me what?"

"I'm afraid you've got quite a lot to do. You're his executor."

3

Why should I see her? She will only want me to give a
message to Albert.

— DISRAELI, 1881, DURING HIS FINAL ILLNESS, ON BEING
TOLD QUEEN VICTORIA PLANNED TO VISIT HIM

SIMON WOULD NEVER HAVE PEGGED DENISE McGRATH AS
David Morgan's sister. The word "scrawny" popped into
his head when he first saw her. She wore nondescript navy
slacks and a blue and tan herringbone blazer. Her hair was
badly cut and frosted, with an inch of brown roots showing. She wore red lipstick and thick powder. Simon remembered that she was younger than Morgan, but he wouldn't
have believed it to look at her. Frown lines knotted her
forehead and dragged the corners of her mouth down to
her chin.

Denise paced up and down the sidewalk outside the
yellow crime scene tape, smoking. Her suitcase rested next
to her on the ground. Simon got out of his car and walked
up to her, extending his hand.

"You're Simon Shaw," she said, taking his hand. "I

would know you anywhere from David's description of you."

Simon could just imagine how David Morgan described him. Small, dark, brilliant, and intense, spared from arrogance by his small-town North Carolina upbringing.

"You, too," Simon lied. Morgan had rarely spoken of Denise and her family, although he wouldn't have expected him to, given his reticent personality. Simon knew that Denise was a high school teacher, her husband was unable to walk more than a few steps, and that they had three young children. Life had been a struggle for them since the traffic accident that disabled her husband.

"Why are you waiting out here?" Simon asked.

"It didn't occur to me that I wouldn't be able to get into the house," Denise said. "But, of course, it's a crime scene. Can't touch anything, can't take anything out of it. The policeman over there"—she gestured with her hand to the uniformed officer sitting on Morgan's porch—"won't let me in to even get the keys to my brother's truck."

"Let me talk to the officer," Simon said. "I have police connections."

THE OFFICER WAS IMPLACABLE.

"The scene has to be officially released before I can let anyone in, Professor Shaw," the policeman said. "The forensics guys took multiple evidence bags out of here yesterday, but they're coming back this afternoon. What with all these television shows on forensics, juries expect miracles. You won't be able to get the access to the house until they've processed every nook and cranny twice."

"But Mrs. McGrath is Dr. Morgan's sister," Simon said.

"She expected to be able to stay here and drive his car. She's got to arrange the funeral and everything."

"I can't do a thing," the policeman said. "And she can't get the body until the autopsy's complete, anyway."

SIMON DROVE DENISE McGRATH to a nearby hotel, where, blessedly, there was a room available. They waited in the lobby for the elevator.

"I guess, considering the circumstances, I'm going to nap for a while," she said. "I've been awake since the police called yesterday morning."

Simon thought she seemed removed from her brother's death, behaving almost as if she were on a business trip.

"I'd like to schedule the funeral as soon as possible," Denise said. "Do you think we could plan it for Thursday?"

"That might be pushing it," Simon said. "There's a lot to do."

"You think I'm callous, don't you?" she asked.

"Of course not," Simon lied.

"Yes, you do," she said, covering her eyes for a second. She wore a wide gold wedding band on her left ring finger, but no diamond. "I loved my brother, but you see, my husband's in a wheelchair most of the time, and we have three children, I've got a friend staying with them, and a substitute teacher taking my classes, and I need to get everything settled and get back home. I don't have the leisure to carry on about all this."

"I'll do whatever I can to help you."

"Oh, I mentioned you were his executor," she said,

pulling an envelope out of her purse. "Here's the copy of the will David sent me, and a letter for you. I'm going to call the police department later this afternoon to see when the body"—and here she hesitated, then pulled herself together—"will be released. I believe that you're the one who starts probate."

"I'll find out what I need to do. You're not to worry about it."

He watched her roll her suitcase onto the elevator. Some people seemed to have more than their share of bad luck.

"YOU DON'T WANT ME to release the scene too soon, Simon, and maybe miss something that would help us catch the murderer, do you?" Gates said over the phone.

"No, of course not," Simon said. "It just seems like one last indignity."

"Don't hold me to this," Gates said, "but maybe we can turn over the keys to you tomorrow, since you're Dr. Morgan's executor. And I want to be there when you first go through the house. You're the person who would be most likely to notice something we might have overlooked."

"Of course."

"You'll want to get a crime scene cleanup company in there first thing," Gates said. "The house is covered in fingerprint powder and luminol, not to mention some body fluids in the office, and it wasn't clean to begin with. I suggest that you give the cleaners the keys as soon as you get them, have them clean before you and Mrs. McGrath go into the house. As crime scenes go it's not grisly, but you don't need to see it." Otis gave Simon the name of a reputable company.

Simon hung up the phone. Nasty business, death.

SIMON READ THE WILL. It was brief and to the point. Denise McGrath inherited all Morgan's money and personal property. His life insurance was directed into his estate to pay funeral and settlement expenses, after which the executor, Simon, would disburse the balance to Denise. Morgan's house was to be sold to fund an educational trust for McGrath's three sons. Simon was the residuary legatee. He inherited whatever personal property Denise didn't want.

"THAT MEANS YOU GET the leftovers," Julia said. She'd just gotten in from work and was still wearing her lawyer clothes, a tailored gray suit, which didn't flatter her at all. She'd twisted her beautiful hair into a French braid.

"Like what?" Simon said.

"Whatever Mrs. McGrath doesn't want," Julia said, "is yours."

All those Stephen King paperbacks.

"Oh."

"As executor, you're responsible for settling the estate. And you're entitled as executor to a fee and expenses. The fee is some percentage of the estate, I believe. Trusts and estates aren't my specialty."

"I won't accept any money."

"You'll want your expenses," she said. "Being an executor can involve a lot of work, even if the estate is simple."

"Great. Just what I need."

"I imagine he wanted to spare his sister the trouble. Oh, and this wasn't drawn up by a lawyer, it's one of those forms you fill out. And it's a photocopy. You'll need to make a good faith search for the original, and make sure there's not a more recent one."

"A good faith search?"

"Yeah, you'll have to go through his house and papers and such."

Terrific. Just what Simon wanted to do right now, paw through Morgan's belongings. If he was lucky enough to meet the man in heaven or wherever someday, he'd have plenty to say to him about all this.

"There's a sealed letter there addressed to me, too, I didn't have the heart to open it," Simon said.

"Want me to read it?"

"Tell you what, just tell me if there's anything in it I need to know right now, and leave it. I'll read the rest later."

Julia gulped from her glass of chardonnay, and Simon drained half of his bourbon, as if in preparation for an ordeal. She removed the letter from the envelope, two sheets covered with Morgan's handwriting.

"Okay," she said after a second. "All you need to know right now is that there's a file in Morgan's home office, in a desk drawer, not one of the file cabinets, that contains all the documents you need. The letter says you can't miss it, and it's supposed to contain the original of the will."

She got up and went over to the mantelpiece and stuck the letter behind a picture of Simon's parents.

"I'll leave it right here, and you can read it when you're ready," she said.

"Thanks," Simon said. He wondered when that would be.

"Hungry?"

"Not at all."

"I got roast chicken, mashed potatoes, and salad from the Fresh Market."

"I'll try."

Julia changed into jeans and a sweater, and came into the kitchen, where Simon was laying supper out on the table. They sat down, and Simon was able to eat a few bites. Julia didn't have any mashed potatoes and just a small piece of chicken. Normally he would have chided her about her dieting, but tonight he didn't have the energy.

Julia looked wonderful. She had a great figure and glossy auburn hair she wore down to her shoulders when she wasn't working. But physically Simon felt nothing. No sex drive, no hunger, no thirst, just a craving for bourbon. Every ounce of his being was focused on getting through the day, hour by interminable hour.

Speaking of bourbon, he needed another one. He went so far as to walk into his dining room and over to the liquor cabinet and open the door. Julia noticed, but didn't say a word.

He stared at the Maker's Mark bottle. If he was going to continue to drink heavily, he needed to find a cheaper brand. He changed his mind about the drink and put the bottle back into the cabinet. He had to be an executor tomorrow. Didn't need a hangover. He went back into the kitchen and sat back down.

"No bender tonight?" Julia asked.

"No. I need what sense I still have to take care of business tomorrow. I hope I can get some sleep."

"I've got some sleeping pills you can take."

THEY SPENT THE REST of the evening quietly. Julia worked out of her briefcase on the coffee table in the living room, while Simon checked the Internet for information on being an executor. Good lord. His duties were endless, starting with opening an estate account, notifying creditors, handling all Morgan's bequests, and accounting for everything to the clerk of court.

"There's a lot of work to be done here," Simon said.

"He trusted you, that's obvious," Julia said.

"I know. I'll do my best."

Julia put down her papers and came and sat on the sofa next to him, put her hands on his shoulders and rubbed his neck.

"I'll help if I can."

"Thanks. Aren't you sick of babysitting me?"

"I can bear it for a few more days."

Simon called Denise McGrath. He explained that as soon as he had the keys to Morgan's house he would call in a crime scene cleanup crew, and after they were done she could stay in the house and use the truck. He assured her that the estate would cover her expenses, the funeral, and Morgan's outstanding bills. He didn't want to promise her more than that yet. Then Simon took one of Julia's pills and went to bed. Tomorrow promised to be a very long day.

"Good morning, Dr. Shaw," the bank teller, one of Simon's old students, at the credit union said, "you're up bright and early. Are you okay? You look like you lost your best friend."

Simon told her he needed to settle the estate of a friend who'd just died, and who kept his accounts at the credit union, and then she covered her face with both hands.

"Oh, my God," she said, "I'm so sorry, I didn't know."

Simon reassured her that it was okay, he wasn't upset, and not to worry, but he was willing to bet she'd never use that expression again.

Simon had already picked up Morgan's death certificate at the morgue. He'd been there before, on one of his cases, and just sitting in the waiting room turned his stomach. Despite the colorful decor, the antiseptic odor, the cheerful receptionist, death hovered there, so palpable you could almost see his bleak aspect crouching in a dark corner. Simon took the death certificate from a pathologist, turned down an opportunity to view Morgan's corpse, and fled.

"We put both yours and Dr. Morgan's name on the account," the young banker said, "and transfer all of the decedent's funds into it. Then you can write checks on it. There's not much, a little less than two thousand dollars."

Not nearly enough for expenses, Simon thought.

"He had life insurance," Simon said.

"When that check comes," he said, "we'll deposit it, too. He was a state employee? That amount is usually one and a half times salary."

"It should be about seventy-five thousand, then," Simon said.

"If you cover any of Dr. Morgan's expenses, save the receipts so you can reimburse yourself. In fact, save every scrap of paper. You have to account for every penny to the clerk of court." He checked his computer again. "Dr. Morgan had no other accounts with us, no IRAs, no safety-deposit box. He did have a truck loan and a mortgage. You can pay off the truck loan after the life insurance check comes. Do you know what you're going to do with the house?"

"It's going to be sold to fund a trust," Simon said.

"The mortgage isn't much," the banker said. "He bought the house fifteen years ago. It should be worth a lot more now, since it's inside the beltline and everything. Remember you have to keep up the mortgage payments, maintenance, and the utility bills until closing."

Simon pondered who he'd select as his executor now that he knew what it entailed. He would choose someone he really disliked, someone who'd earned the stress and work it entailed. Definitely not his best friend, who deserved much better from him. Like a small personal bequest to cover bourbon and sleeping pills.

He thought about Morgan's estate as he drove to the state Human Resources Department, where he'd apply for Morgan's life insurance. He figured he could write a check for half of it to give to Denise McGrath as soon as he received it, then give her the rest after the estate was settled. He doubted Morgan owed money on anything other than his car loan and mortgage.

"Don't forget his retirement account," the woman at

Human Resources said. "Do you know who the beneficiary is?"

Simon had forgotten about the state retirement plan.

"Not a clue," he said.

"The real value of the state retirement fund is in retirement benefits. The actual monetary value if someone dies
before retiring is the amount of his contributions, plus a bit
of interest." She checked her computer. "The beneficiary is
Denise McGrath, a sister?" she said. "She'll get around
forty thousand dollars, I expect."

If Morgan's estate held no surprise debts, Denise
should inherit about a hundred thousand dollars, and the
house maybe would clear fifty thousand for her children's
education. Not a fortune, but not chicken feed, either.

To Simon's surprise, the woman said he could pick up
Morgan's life insurance check by the end of the week. The
retirement account would take longer to process and the
funds would be sent directly to Mrs. McGrath.

To Simon's relief, he was able to get the keys to the
house by mid-morning and engage the You Can Count on
Us crime scene cleanup company to work immediately.

"I'll meet you at the house this afternoon" Gates said
as he handed over the keys. "Don't you and Mrs. McGrath
go inside until I get there. I want your first impressions."

SIMON CALLED JULIA AT work and asked her to lunch, on
the condition that she order something other than salad.
He was descended from a long line of Jewish women and
he liked to see people eat. They decided against their
favorite restaurant, Irregardless Café, since it reminded

both of them of their earlier, more intimate friendship, and went to Frazier's.

"You need to shave first," Julia said, "and change your shirt. I'm surprised they let you into that bank without frisking you."

Simon still wasn't hungry, but he was able to eat a little of the steak he ordered. Julia had salmon and a diet soda.

"Am I doing everything right?" Simon asked, after he'd recounted his morning.

"I think so. Since you're the executor, and his employee life insurance is directed into his estate, you can use that at your discretion to pay all the bills, then give the remainder to Denise. She's the beneficiary of the retirement account, so that amount goes directly to her. Over the next few days, encourage her to decide what personal property she wants to keep."

"I hate this," Simon said.

"Actually, I think it's helping you cope. Gives you something to do. Has Denise mentioned the funeral?"

"It's tomorrow afternoon. The body's been released."

At that point, any semblance of an appetite abandoned Simon, and he passed on dessert.

After lunch the two of them drove past Morgan's house. A white unmarked van was parked in the driveway. Two men wearing white jumpsuits were setting up large cardboard boxes in the front yard and lining them with orange plastic bags. Another went inside lugging cleaning supplies and an industrial vacuum cleaner. Simon didn't stop.

————

AFTER THE CLEANING COMPANY finished its work, Simon picked up Denise McGrath at her hotel and drove to Morgan's house, with a stop at a coffee shop on the way. Denise requested a latte with skim milk, Simon ordered black coffee for Otis, and he got a large with lots of cream and sugar for himself.

Otis wasn't at the house yet when they arrived, so while they waited in the car, Simon told Denise about the money that should come her way.

"Oh, my God," she said, stunned, leaning on the arm of the car door for support. "I didn't think. I mean, I knew the kids and I would inherit, but I didn't think there'd be much cash. Oh, my God. That will get us just about even—it will take care of our medical and credit card bills."

At least some good would come out of Morgan's death, Simon thought.

Otis drove up, got out of the car, and gratefully accepted the coffee Simon had gotten him. They paused outside the door.

"Remember," Gates said, "I want you to check carefully around the house. Tell me if you notice anything unusual, anything at all."

"Well," Simon said, as they walked into the front room, "it's clean."

"Other than that," Gates said.

They went quietly through every room in the house: the eighties-era galley kitchen, which for once didn't have dishes in the sink; the living room, furnished with a comfortable sofa, a battered recliner, and a big-screen television; the patio off the living room, swept clean of leaves;

Morgan's bedroom, which contained a chest of drawers, a double bed, and a bookcase full of paperbacks; and the spare room, furnished with unmade twin beds, a bedside table, and a lamp. Finally they went into Morgan's office.

What was missing was obvious. An entire shelf was bare. Simon turned to Otis.

"That was full of mementos and artifacts."

Otis nodded. "We thought something must have occupied that shelf. Every other nook is crammed. What was there?"

Simon had a photographic memory.

"Two Paleo-Indian pots," he said. "A stone pipe. A Folsom spear point. And the murder weapon."

4

I have spent a lot of time searching through the Bible for
loopholes.

—W. C. FIELDS (1880–1946), SAID DURING HIS LAST ILLNESS

"IT WAS A GEODE," SIMON SAID, "A BIG ONE," spreading his
hands about eight inches apart. "Amethyst quartz." A
geode was a rock bubble lined with crystals, split in half
for display. Morgan had picked his up in the western part
of the state years ago.

"You could be right," Gates said. "The round half of a
large geode fits the description of the murder weapon. It
would sure be hard enough and heavy enough to do the
job. Do you think you'd recognize this one if you saw it
again?"

"I doubt it," Simon said. "I mean, it was a beautiful
object, but I don't think I could distinguish it from another
one the same size and color."

"Notice anything else unusual?"

Simon scanned the desk.

"I don't see his laptop."

"The forensic computer boys have it down at the station. His briefcase is there, too. It was on the floor next to the desk."

Otis starting punching in numbers on his cell phone before he'd finished his sentence.

"Hold on," he said to one of his detectives on the other end of the phone. "The stuff that's missing," he said to Simon, "was it valuable?"

Simon shook his head. "No, not really."

Otis went out into the hall to finish his conversation. Simon knew he would be ordering a new search of the area around Morgan's house now that he had a description of a possible murder weapon.

He slumped into the chair at Morgan's desk. The desk, clear except for a lamp, a couple of cheap ballpoint pens, and a pristine yellow legal pad, faced into the room, with a window and the door leading to the back yard behind it. A bad arrangement if you wanted to avoid being brained from the rear. Simon shook the thought out of his head, and focused on inspecting the room where his friend had been killed.

Morgan was as neat and organized about his work as he was untidy and careless in his personal life. Alphabetized books, all relating to archaeology and the prehistory of North Carolina, filled two mismatched bookshelves. A third bookshelf, constructed of cinder blocks and boards, like the one Simon built in his college dorm room, contained stack after stack of periodicals and journals. Morgan was a keeper, not a shredder. A row of mismatched metal file cabinets stood against another wall. Simon figured that Denise wouldn't want the books and files, so he'd have to deal with them. What in God's name would he do with it all?

Simon could hear Gates's voice in the hall, still on his call to his office, and the sound of Denise in the living room, opening cabinets and moving stuff about. What was she doing? Taking inventory? She went into the kitchen and he heard the refrigerator door open. If Denise wanted water, she wouldn't find any of the fancy bottled kind. Morgan drank his water straight from the tap, usually out of an unwashed coffee mug.

Simon sat down at the desk and circled his emotional wagons before he opened the desk drawer. When he did, he saw a manila envelope embellished with a crudely drawn skull. Morgan's idea of humor, sketched without really comprehending its effect on Simon should he actually see it one day. Simon tore open the long brown envelope and extracted a short note addressed to Simon, the original of Morgan's over-the-counter will, and another life insurance policy. Simon studied the policy. It was additional to the insurance Morgan had from his employer and benefited his sister Denise McGrath, to the tune of two hundred and fifty thousand dollars. It looked as though Morgan had bought the additional insurance about the time of Denise's husband's car accident. He was providing, as best he could, for his sister and her kids.

Simon opened the note. *Hey Simon, if you're reading this, I must have fallen off a cliff or succumbed to the smokes. Sorry about the executor stuff. Please take whatever fee you're entitled to and go down the Nile or something after the estate's settled. Oh, and if Denise will let you, dispense with the formalities. You know I hate funerals. Just stir my ashes into the sand in the cigarette ash can outside Players' Retreat.*

Simon couldn't bear to look at his friend's signature. He felt sick and cold to his core. He stuffed the papers back into the envelope, leaned his elbows on the desk, and rested his head in his hands.

"You okay?" Gates asked, coming back into the office.

"Sure," Simon said. He held up the envelope. "I found the will," he said. "It's the original of the copy his sister gave me. And another life insurance policy."

"How much?" Gates asked, instantly focused.

"Two hundred fifty thousand dollars," Simon said, "and she can use it."

"She's the only heir?"

"I'm the residuary legatee," Simon said. "Whatever personal property she doesn't want, I get."

"How much, total, do you think the estate's worth?"

Simon calculated. "The house money goes into a trust for her kids. Maybe fifty thousand? And she'll get, with the rest of the insurance and the retirement account, say, four hundred thousand."

"You implied that she needs the money?"

Simon didn't much like what Gates was thinking.

"Her husband's disabled. They're living on her salary as a teacher, and they've got three young kids. They're struggling."

"Money," Gates said, thumbing through the papers, "the purest motive of all."

"You can't be serious," Simon said. "She's his sister."

"So?" Gates handed the policy back to Simon. "I think you should tell Mrs. McGrath about her good fortune right now. I want to see her reaction."

The two of them went into the living room, furnished in the eighties from a discount store and forgotten since. Denise was sitting on the black vinyl sofa, smoking a cigarette, her bony legs crossed, staring out the sliding glass door into the back yard.

When Simon spoke to her, she started.

"Sorry," she said, and stubbed out her cigarette into an ashtray, uncommonly clean because of the crime scene janitors. "I was thinking about my brother."

Simon sat down next to her on the sofa. Gates settled into Morgan's bulky recliner.

"I found the original will in Morgan's desk," Simon said. "The terms are the same as the copy you gave me. The profits from the house go into a trust for your kids, and you get the life insurance and any of the personal property you want."

"The life insurance is seventy-five thousand, like you said in the car?" she asked. "And the retirement account is about forty thousand?"

Gates leaned imperceptibly toward her. It made Simon uncomfortable, as if he was grilling Denise without her knowledge on behalf of the police. He resented Gates for asking him to do it.

"I found an additional policy in the desk," Simon said. "For two hundred fifty thousand dollars. You're the beneficiary."

Denise clapped her hands over her mouth, staring at him. Then one hand went to her chest and the other gripped the arm of the sofa.

"Oh, my God!" she said. "I don't believe it! I had no idea!"

Simon handed her the policy. "All you need to do is fill out the forms, include a copy of the death certificate, and send it all in to the company."

Denise began to cry loudly and messily. Fat tears rolled down her cheeks, etching gutters in the thick powder that coated her face. Gates got up and went outside through the glass doors onto the patio, ostensibly to give them privacy, where he lit a cigarette himself, but he left the door cracked so he could hear their conversation. Simon couldn't find any tissue, so he ripped off a handful of toilet paper in the bathroom and brought it back to Denise. She dabbed at her face and blew her nose.

Then she reached out a hand for the policy.

"You don't know what this will mean to my family," she said.

"It looks like Morgan took the insurance out shortly after your husband was injured," Simon said.

Denise gulped, forcing back more tears.

"He's been sending me money since the accident," she said. "I've got to wash my face." She got up off the sofa and went into the bathroom.

Simon sucked in a couple of heavy breaths. This was hard, very hard.

By the time Denise returned, Gates was back in the living room. She had fully recovered her poise and repaired her makeup. She picked the policy up off the sofa where she had left it and stuffed it in her purse.

"How soon can I get a copy of the death certificate?" she asked.

"I've got the certificate at home," Simon said. "I'll make a copy and bring it to you."

"Maybe I can get this in the mail today," Denise said, checking her watch. "I wonder if it needs to be notarized."

"There's a notary at the credit union where Morgan banked," Simon said. "Right down the street."

"Do you still need me, Sergeant?" Denise said to Gates. "I've never been in my brother's house before, so I can't tell you anything about what's missing. I'd like to go to my hotel and call my husband and check out."

"Of course," Gates said.

"Keys," she said, turning to Simon.

"What?"

"The keys to my brother's truck and to the house."

"Oh, sure," Simon said. "He kept a set hanging over here." Simon lifted them off a hook in the kitchen and handed them to her. He kept the set Gates had given him. He was the executor, and he wanted to go through the house again, without the police this time.

"Is it new? The truck, I mean," she asked.

"It's a couple of years old," Simon said. "He took good care of it."

"I'll keep it, then," she said. "I'm sure my local dealer can remove the winch and fog lights. Don't know if I want the camper, though, I doubt my husband could get in and out of it."

She left the house, backed Morgan's beloved black Ford F-150 pickup down the driveway, and drove off toward her hotel.

"WELL, WELL," GATES SAID.

"I'm sure Denise was home with her family or at work when her brother died."

"I intend to find out."

"She didn't know about the two hundred and fifty thousand dollars," Simon said. "You could tell by her reaction."

"Maybe not. But she knew she was her brother's heir, and she expected some money from him should he die."

"You can't seriously consider her a suspect," Simon said.

"Of course I do," Gates said. "And you would, too, if you weren't so emotionally involved. Look, I'm the policeman, you're the family friend. Period. I know you've done some damn good detective work in the past. But you must stay clear of this investigation. It's not one of your historical cold cases. This is now, today, the present, and the murderer is still out there, and likely very dangerous. It's no job for an amateur. Understand?"

Otis rested his hand on Simon's shoulder. It was a sincere, friendly gesture, but Simon knew Otis would back up his advice with action if he thought Simon was overstepping his bounds. Otis was being polite and considerate, but his meaning was clear. Simon was locked out of the official investigation into Morgan's murder.

"Sure, of course," Simon said. What else could he say?

Simon watched Otis drive away in his old Cadillac, then he locked up Morgan's house. Denise would soon be back from her hotel to live in the house until after the funeral, but he still felt as if he were screwing down the lid of a coffin.

Simon was well aware that he was naive to believe that Denise couldn't be responsible for Morgan's murder. He simply did not want his friend to have been killed by his sister. That was the nasty stuff of daytime talk shows, and Morgan's memory deserved better.

Simon turned to see Morgan's next-door neighbor standing on the sidewalk out front with a woman he didn't recognize. The neighbor was a retired high school teacher who'd volunteered at the state archaeology research lab. Simon had talked to him a few times during basketball game nights at Morgan's. The woman was in her sixties, hair expertly frosted, wearing khaki trousers, pristine white walking shoes, and diamond solitaire earrings.

"Hi," Simon said to the neighbor, reaching out his hand. "You're Don White, I believe?"

"That's right," White said. "And I'd like you to meet Mrs. Angela Grove. She's a neighbor, too. We want you to know how sorry we are."

"Thanks," Simon said.

"And we were just wondering," Mrs. Grove said, "if you knew what would happen to Dr. Morgan's house?"

Simon was so familiar with inside-the-beltline fever that he wasn't surprised that they would ask about the house. Hardly was a homeowner cold in this part of town, much less in the grave, before speculation began over the value or sale of his or her home. How much was it worth? Would the heirs keep it? Would the buyer knock it down and build a megamansion with media room and gourmet kitchen and no yard? Would the new owners have children, big dogs, or convert the garage into an office? Might the heirs, God forbid, rent it to North Carolina State students?

"It will be sold to fund a trust," Simon said. "After probate, of course. I'm the executor."

"You see," Mrs. Grove said, "my daughter and her husband have been looking in this neighborhood for a couple of years now. Perhaps a private sale could be arranged? It would save the estate a Realtor's commission. And I assure you our financial references are excellent."

Simon bit his tongue.

"This is very premature," Simon said. "I don't know how I'm going to handle the sale yet."

"I understand," Mrs. Grove said, whipping out a business card with her name and telephone number on it. Simon took it. She was a party planner and cake decorator. "Perhaps you could call me?"

"I'll see," Simon said. "And I'd appreciate it if you wouldn't tell anyone else I'm Dr. Morgan's executor." Simon didn't need frenzied house hunters and real estate agents calling him at all hours.

Simon opened his car door, effectively closing the conversation.

"We're truly sorry about Dr. Morgan," White said. "He was a good man. Let me know if I can help you with anything."

ON HIS DRIVE HOME to pick up Morgan's death certificate, Simon reflected on his conversation with Sophie and Marcus, when they'd speculated on what Morgan owned that could be considered valuable. Gates would proceed with the two obvious possible motives for the murder, that Morgan was killed for his estate, or as a result of a robbery gone bad. It was his job to be practical about searching for the murderer. But what if Morgan wasn't murdered for the classic reasons? Despite the respect he had for Otis Gates and his detective abilities, Simon didn't think the sergeant appreciated the intensity of the dispute over the disposition of Uwharrie Man, or the impact a decision on the skeleton's fate would have on the careers of the interested parties. There was no more vicious political environment than academia, and Simon was uniquely qualified to pene-trate it.

SIMON WAITED IN LINE for a copy machine at the copy center. He stood behind an elderly woman with a cane and a heap of medical insurance forms and a student clutching an armful of notes. The mundane quality of the scene irritated him. He was here to make copies of his best friend's death certificate, for God's sake. Didn't these people realize how close they were to disaster? One phone call could ruin their lives, yet they were preoccupied with bills and schoolwork.

He went back to Morgan's house to find Denise already there, sitting at the kitchen table with a stack of papers, filling out forms. She looked like a new woman. Amazing what news of a big inheritance could do for a person's appearance. As good as going to a spa.

Denise seized the death certificate Simon handed to her and stuffed it into a waiting envelope, already addressed and stamped. She was so organized she'd stopped at the post office on her way to the house.

"Did you find a notary?" Simon asked.

"Sure did," Denise said. "I'll drop this in the mail later. Do you want something to eat?" she asked, gesturing toward Morgan's refrigerator. "People are already dropping off food. There's a ham and sandwich stuff in the refrigerator. And a chocolate cake."

"No thanks," Simon said. "I had a big lunch."

"Two gorgeous bouquets of flowers have been delivered," Denise said. "A dozen yellow roses, and one with white chrysanthemums and orchids. They're still in the florist's containers because I couldn't find a decent vase in the house."

Morgan hadn't been a collector of vases.

"And David's secretary called," Denise said. "She wants to help with the funeral and the reception afterward. Since I don't know anyone here, I accepted, with relief. She's coming over later tonight to help me write the obituary."

Simon had been waiting for an opportunity to bring up the funeral. "Morgan didn't want a funeral," Simon said. "He said so in his note to me. He wanted to be cremated and his ashes scattered." Simon didn't mention the cigarette ash urn outside Players' Retreat, that ageless dive, in the best sense of the word, across from North Carolina State, where the management permitted smoking. Morgan spent at least two nights a week there, eating greasy hamburgers, drinking beer, playing pool, or watching a ball game on the television in a back room.

Denise shook her head. "Cremation is out of the question," she said. "I know my brother didn't believe, but I wouldn't be living up to my responsibility if I didn't see that he had a proper Christian funeral and burial."

She looked around the room.

"Do you see my purse?"

"On the counter next to the sink," Simon said.

"I'm off, then," she said, grabbing up her purse and waving the envelope addressed to the insurance company.

Simon didn't want to be angry with Denise. Morgan was dead, nothing could be done about that, and Denise's inheritance solved all her financial problems, but she didn't have to seem so blissfully relieved. She could at least pretend to be grieving for the next few days. When she got home, out of Simon's sight, then she could turn cartwheels over her windfall.

Simon went back to Morgan's office and found the file he was looking for under *Uwharrie Man, Committee for the Disposition of*, in one of Morgan's filing cabinets. There was a second file right behind it, *Uwharrie Man, Research*. Both bulged with papers. Simon removed both files and took them out to his car.

SEVERAL FOOD PARCELS AND a bunch of flowers waited for Simon on his front porch. Neighbors had dropped off casseroles conveniently packaged in disposable containers. The flowers, wrapped in wet newspaper to keep them fresh, were anonymous, but Simon recognized the spiky yellow spider mums and copper button mums from the garden of a neighbor down the street.

Inside, he put the food in the refrigerator and found in the upper reaches of a kitchen cabinet a dusty cut-crystal vase that once belonged to his parents. He washed it out, put the flowers in it, and set the vase on the black Steinway baby grand piano in his living room.

Simon went back into the kitchen and carefully measured a jigger of bourbon, poured it over ice, then filled the glass to the brink with Coke. He'd never drunk this mixture before Morgan's death, but he found that the booze for his nerves and the Coke for his stomach was a good combination. While he sipped, he leafed through Morgan's research files on Uwharrie Man.

The discovery of Uwharrie Man lit a fire under the archaeological community in North Carolina. Until then, no remains of human beings had been found that dated before the late Paleo-Indian era, or about 10,000 BP. This date excluded North Carolina from the most interesting and contentious issues in American prehistory, like who got here first, when did they arrive, and just how important was it, anyway?

Simon had a basic understanding of the fundamentals of human prehistory, gleamed mostly from late-night Discovery Channel marathons. Modern humans, curious and adaptable animals, left Africa about sixty to eighty thousand years ago and spread rapidly around the world. Their offspring colonized Asia by 50,000 BP and Europe by 40,000 BP. Those humans who colonized the Asian subcontinent over time evolved Mongoloid features. Then a few Asian clans settled in the forbidding climate of Siberia. They hunted megafauna like the woolly mammoth, built huts with mammoth tusk struts thatched with fur, made bone and stone tools, and preserved food in ice pits. One of their settlements, excavated at Yana, Siberia, was over thirty thousand years old.

In college, Simon absorbed the traditional thinking about human migration into the Americas, which presumed that Ice Age glaciers, which covered most of Canada and Alaska, prevented people from moving farther east until a land bridge opened around thirteen thousand years ago. All anthropological, genetic, and linguistic evidence indicated that the American Indian tribes that the Europeans encountered when they landed in America descended from Asians who crossed the Bering Strait land bridge in three waves.

These immigrants quickly invented the Clovis culture, named after a town in Arizona where their oversized, bifaced spear points were first excavated. They were efficient hunters. The Colombian mammoth, giant ground sloth, and cave bear, to name just a few, became extinct within the following thousand years, strong evidence for a major influx of human beings about this time. The earliest date of 10,000 BP for the Hardaway site in North Carolina, until the discovery of Uwharrie Man, fell neatly into the Bering Strait scenario, because it allowed the necessary several thousand years for humans to move from the west coast to the east.

The ultimate success of the Bering Strait immigrants didn't exclude other arrivals. Humans from other cultures could have found themselves on the American continent, some much earlier than the Siberian explorers. Perhaps they arrived by sea from the east or west, or over an Alaskan land bridge that had formed thousands of years earlier during a previous ice age.

Early-entry advocates point to an unverified site in Monte Verde, Chile, which dated to thirty-three thousand years ago, a possible eighteen-thousand-year-old Nebraska mammoth kill, and sites in South Carolina and Virginia that some think could be fifteen or sixteen thousand years old. Complicating the issue even more, remains of humans who appear not to be Mongoloid have been unearthed in America, most famously Kennewick man, who died over nine thousand years ago, and whose remains were discovered in a streambed in the Pacific Northwest. When Kennewick Man's skull was reconstructed, he looked Caucasoid.

North Carolina got to participate in the excitement after July 2001, when Dr. Lawrence Mabry and his team found Uwharrie Man, whose skeleton lay associated with pre-Clovis points and a fourteen-thousand-year-old hearth in an undisturbed area across Badin Lake from the Hardaway site. Uwharrie Man couldn't have been descended from people who crossed the land bridge thirteen thousand years ago, so he became evidence for the earlier entry advocates.

Mabry and his crew excavated Uwharrie Man and transported him to a special laboratory at the Museum of Natural Sciences in Raleigh. Mabry quickly applied for and received a sizeable grant for the purpose of studying Uwharrie Man, so the Office of State Archaeology, always short of money, officially delegated the analysis of his remains to Mabry and to the museum. But Uwharrie Man hadn't been touched since. Shortly after his bones arrived at the museum, the Lumbee nation, led by Brad Lowery, a member of the Lumbee Tribal Council, claimed that the remains were those of a Native American burial, and as such should be reburied immediately, as required by North Carolina and federal law.

Mabry and the museum faction insisted a skeleton as old as Uwharrie Man couldn't be considered a burial, or an ancestor of any modern tribe, while Lowery and his allies just as adamantly claimed that Uwharrie Man was a Native American, died in land once inhabited by Lumbee ancestor tribes, and had gear with him that could be interpreted as grave goods. They insisted it was sacrilegious to do anything to Uwharrie Man other than rebury him. To reach a compromise, the North Carolina Department of Cultural Resources appointed an Archaeological Advisory Committee. Mabry and Henry Klett, executive director of the museum, expressed the pro-study position; Lowery and Brenda Lambert, the commissioner of Indian affairs, advocated for Native American interests; and David Morgan represented the Office of State Archaeology. Until he was murdered.

Most of the committee file was taken up by Mabry's résumé. Every degree, every award, every speech, every panel membership, and every printed word the man churned out was listed on nearly thirty pages. Simon wanted to gag. Mabry couldn't have collected all that glory without neglecting his undergraduate teaching and abusing his graduate students. Simon's own résumé was one page long, with his publications and such available on request.

The file held two agendas for two meetings in the previous month, but no minutes of either. In fact, there were no notes at all in either file. Knowing Morgan as he had, Simon would have expected each file to contain a letter-sized three-hole-punched yellow legal pad, covered with copious notes. There weren't even any comments in the margins of the documents in the research file. From looking through the files, Simon had no idea what Morgan's opinion was about the disposition of Uwharrie Man, or what was going on in the committee. Flipping back through the agendas, Simon noticed that a meeting had been scheduled for today, at three o'clock. Surely it would have been canceled. Wouldn't it? He reached for the telephone.

5

"Dying," he said to me, "is a very dull, dreary affair."
Suddenly he smiled. "And my advice to you is to have
nothing whatever to do with it," he added.

—SOMERSET MAUGHAM, SHORTLY BEFORE HIS DEATH IN
1965, AS RECORDED BY HIS NEPHEW, ROBIN MAUGHAM

HENRY KLETT MET SIMON OUTSIDE THE DOUBLE DOORS OF
his office off a corridor of the North Carolina Museum of
Natural Sciences, just around a corner from the third-floor
atrium that corralled a rearing, roaring dinosaur, Acrocan-
thosaurus, whose nickname was "Terror of the South."
When Simon reached out his hand, Klett clasped it in both
of his.

"Of course we canceled today's meeting," Klett said. "I
am so terribly sorry about Dr. Morgan. What an awful
thing. I liked him very much. Do the police know what
happened yet?"

"No," Simon said, "I'm afraid not."

Klett released Simon's hand with a final squeeze.
"Come in and let's talk," he said, ushering Simon back into
his office. "Can I get you anything? Water?"

"If you have a cold Coke, I'd take it," Simon said.

Most state government offices were less than luxurious. But according to a plaque posted on the wall outside the door of Klett's office, his had been furnished through the fund-raising efforts of the Friends of the North Carolina State Museums. The plaque appeased those taxpayers who might be annoyed by the elegance of the space. The refined surroundings made sense to Simon, for Klett had to deal with wealthy donors and eminent scientists.

Simon sat in one of the two leather wing chairs that faced Klett's desk while Klett fetched him a Coke from a small refrigerator hidden in a bank of mahogany shelves and cupboards. Simon had met Klett before, and found him to be an interesting mix of politician and scientist. He'd spearheaded the drive to build the new museum, which meant he was comfortable raising money and schmoozing with donors and legislators, but he'd also organized some remarkable exhibits. He was a fit man with a full head of gray hair, carefully dressed in a blue suit and a silk tie. Simon suddenly remembered that he hadn't shaved today, and that he was wearing a shirt he'd picked up off his bedroom floor. He smoothed back his hair, straightened his jacket, and hoped he didn't look too disreputable.

"So, what can I do to help you, Dr. Shaw?" Klett asked.

"I'm David Morgan's executor," Simon said. "I'm handling his affairs. I have some questions about his service on the Uwharrie Man committee. I don't suppose you're obliged to answer them, but I would appreciate it."

"Of course," Klett said. "I can understand that you'd be curious. It's an important issue, and I hope you don't mind me saying that Dr. Morgan's death, besides being very sad, of course, could prove to be a problem for us."

"I didn't see any minutes of the committee meetings in the files," Simon said.

"Oh, yes," Klett said. "That's because we called them organizational meetings, not official meetings, and I decided not to publish minutes. That was my idea, actually, I thought the discussions were too acrimonious to document. As a historian you can appreciate that once words are committed to paper, or bytes for that matter, they can't be retracted. I hoped when everyone settled down we could go about recording the discussions and reaching a decision."

"Acrimonious?"

"Yes. Please keep this to yourself, but there was name-calling. And raised voices."

"Between Lawrence Mabry and Brad Lowery?"

"Yes, I was actually worried that one of them might strike the other. After our first meeting I made sure a security guard was posted outside the door to the conference room."

"How uncomfortable."

"I'll say. Brenda Lambert and I have our opinions, too, but years of experience in state government have taught us to express ourselves in a much less confrontational manner."

"Ms. Lambert is allied with Lowery, and you with Dr. Mabry, though, I assume."

"Yes. I support the scientific purpose of this museum, and Ms. Lambert must represent her constituency."

"It seems that my friend was right in the middle of it all."

"That was obvious from the beginning. His vote would have been the tie-breaker."

"Did he say how he intended to vote?"

"Not at all. He didn't say much, period. Just took lots of notes."

"Notes?"

"Yes. He was on his way to filling up a yellow legal pad."

Notes that Simon couldn't find.

Klett hesitated, then leaned forward. "Tell me, Dr. Shaw, if you're Dr. Morgan's executor, then you'd have access to his office, wouldn't you?"

"Yes," Simon said.

"Do you suppose you could look for those notes? If we had a clear idea what Dr. Morgan was thinking, it might help the remaining four of us reach a compromise. Otherwise the governor will appoint a new member to replace Dr. Morgan, and we'd have to start all over again."

"Better the devil you know," Simon said.

"Exactly."

"I'll tell you what," Simon said. "I'll look for those notes. I have to clean out Morgan's office anyway. Might as well be sooner rather than later."

Simon didn't say he'd already been through some of Morgan's files and hadn't found any notes. It seemed wise to keep that to himself for now.

"By the way," Klett said, "would you like to see him?"

"Who?"

"Uwharrie Man. And I saw Dr. Mabry's car in the parking lot this morning. He must be here today too."

"I'd like to meet Dr. Mabry very much," Simon said, "and make the acquaintance of Uwharrie Man."

———

"HERE HE IS," KLETT said, flicking on the lights in a basement laboratory. "Like any celebrity, he's got the best of everything, including climate control."

Despite his detective avocation, Simon avoided human remains and autopsies, preferring to leave them to the experts, but he had visited the Raleigh morgue a couple of times. The long stainless steel table occupying the center of the room, with a large fluorescent light fixture centered over it, reminded him of those visits.

Klett pointed out the glass-topped, coffin-shaped vault against the far wall. Simon peered into it.

"This is not what I'd call a skeleton," Simon said, "this is what I'd call a few old bones."

What must have been the prehistoric man's cranium was just a lump of rock, placed at the head of a few brown sticks. Simon had to use all his imagination to conjure a vaguely skeletal shape, a few ribs and vertebrae, incomplete arms, half of one pelvis, and the bones of one leg.

"I know, but you and I are not as skilled as some," Klett said.

Klett flicked on all the lights in the vast room.

The skeleton rested in the midst of a modern, self-contained archaeology laboratory. Simon recognized some of the equipment shrouded under heavy plastic—a microscopy workstation, a drafting and illustration table, a drying oven, and two computer stations. Specimen drawers lined one wall.

"Dr. Mabry wrote the grant that paid for all this," Klett said. "It's been here for two years, unused. And I've got pledges for an exhibit space, too. The donors are restless, wondering if it will ever happen."

"It must be frustrating," Simon said.

"It is," Klett said. "I mean, the statute the Lumbee invoked to get possession of the skeleton is meant to prevent looting from postcontact Native American burial sites. This man lived in deep time, seven hundred generations ago. He's not anybody's grandfather. If we turn him over to the Lumbee, it would be like emptying museums all over the world of their Neanderthal remains and burying them in caves in Europe. We'd have to ship mummies back to Egypt and seal them up in tombs in the Valley of the Kings with all their grave goods. It's crazy."

Simon wanted to stay neutral, so he changed the subject.

"Can I see the spear point?" he asked. "Morgan said it's beautiful."

"Of course," Klett said. He drew on white cotton gloves, put on a face mask, handed Simon one, and opened one of the specimen drawers. Carefully he lifted the fourteen-thousand-year-old spearhead out of its felt niche. Skillfully fluted and crafted, notched where it would have been secured to a spear with gut and pitch, it was a remarkable object.

"This is the only pre-Clovis point in North Carolina found with human bones and a hearth."

"So the bones have been carbon-dated?" Simon asked.

Klett shook his head. "No," he said, "we don't think we'll be able to date the skeleton. It's been contaminated by groundwater. It's the charcoal from the hearth that's given us the date of fourteen thousand BP. Of course, the skeleton can tell us much more than its age. And then there's the spear point, it's definitely pre-Clovis, a bit shorter and broader than Clovis. It's flint, though there's not a lot of flint in North Carolina. Mabry thinks the stone was quarried in Virginia or South Carolina. There was more trade among prehistoric people than you might think. The Clovis culture appeared, at the earliest, about twelve thousand years ago, so Uwharrie Man must have lived before then. There's just no way around that." Klett carefully replaced the point in its padded drawer and closed it.

"Fourteen thousand years ago is too early for Uwharrie Man to be a descendant of the last Bering Strait migration," Simon said.

"Exactly," Klett said. "All dates in prehistory are relative, of course, ready to be shot to hell by the next discovery. But given that this is the earliest human by far to be found in North Carolina, where did he come from? And how did he get here?"

"France," came a voice from the back of the room. "By water."

"Dr. Shaw," Klett said to Simon, "meet Dr. Lawrence Mabry, the discoverer of Uwharrie Man."

"Actually, my graduate student, Martha Dunn, found him," Mabry said, shaking Simon's hand. "But I led the team."

No man Mabry's age could have real hair that looked like his. It had to be woven to be so thick, and dyed ink-black to boot. And he wore black from head to foot—black slacks, black polo shirt, black Gucci loafers. Mabry tilted his head back slightly to look at Simon, as if he wore contact lenses. God spare me from trying to look thirty-five when I'm pushing sixty, Simon thought.

"Dr. Mabry believes Uwharrie Man arrived on our shores from France," Klett said. "Or rather, his ancestors did."

"His parent culture was Solutrean," Mabry said, "a culture that produced assemblages very similar to American pre-Clovis. Originated about twenty thousand years ago in France."

"How did he get here?" Simon asked.

"By boat," Mabry said. "He, or rather his forebears, followed the edge of the ice sheet across the Atlantic, fishing, hunting walrus and seal along the way. There's plenty of evidence that prehistoric humans were competent boatmen."

"Very interesting theory," Simon said.

"That's all it will be, a theory, unless we can examine his skeleton and the rest of the materials," Mabry said. "The idea of reburying it is preposterous crap. Politically motivated. That fool Lowery wants to get to Congress, and Brenda Lambert wants to keep the natives happy."

"Christ, Larry, be quiet," Klett said, laying a hand on Mabry's arm.

"And if Uwharrie Man is Caucasian, then the Indians exterminated a white culture that settled here before they did. They'd lose their precious status as the first Americans."

Klett rolled his eyes upward.

"It's the truth, damn it, and besides, no one can hear us," Mabry said.

"Simon has offered to look for Dr. Morgan's notes," Klett said, distracting Mabry from his rant.

"Thank God," Mabry said. "I'm sure Dr. Morgan would have agreed with us. He was a true scientist, we all respected him immensely. If we could find out for sure that he intended to vote with us, we could perhaps convince the governor and avoid starting our discussions all over again. I don't think my blood pressure could stand it, not to mention my sponsors."

"I haven't found any notes in the obvious places, but he kept everything," Simon said. "Since I am his executor, I need to go through his office anyway. I'll do it as quickly as I can."

"I would be happy to send my graduate student to help," Mabry said. "She has a lot at stake here. She's writing her dissertation on Uwharrie Man."

What an awful position to be in, Simon thought. If the Lumbee reburied the skeleton, she'd lose years of work. The halls of academia were littered with the bones of graduate students whose dissertations were sabotaged by events not under their control. He needed to meet Martha Dunn.

"I'm going to be packing up Morgan's office later today," Simon said. "If you think she'd really like to help."

"I'll call her right now," Mabry said. "She'll be there, I promise you."

Simon was turning the key in the ignition of his Thunderbird before he realized that Mabry hadn't said he was sorry about Morgan's death.

SOMEONE HAD THOUGHTFULLY LEFT a foam ice chest half full of ice on Simon's front porch to hold the funerary offerings left for him: an angel food cake, a tuna casserole, a loaf of freshly baked bread, and a baking dish of macaroni and cheese. There was enough food in his refrigerator for him to live on for a week, eating much better than he usually did.

Marianne Clegg, Marcus's wife, had dropped off a bunch of autumn foliage from their farm with a note.

Simon found a large tarnished silver water pitcher, another relic of his parents' life, under a counter, stuck the arrangement in it, and left it on his fireplace mantel. His living room was beginning to look like someone had died.

SIMON WAS SIPPING ON a bourbon on ice when Julia got home. She raised an eyebrow at him.

"It's six o'clock and this is my first," Simon said, omitting the drink he'd had at lunch, since lunchtime felt like days ago.

"Whatever you say. So, what are we doing for dinner? I'm starving."

"There's food in the refrigerator," Simon said. "Someone left an ice chest on the porch so people could drop stuff off."

"Let me change."

Simon refreshed his drink while she was out of the room. This was not a sign of impending alcoholism, he told himself. Lots of people occasionally had three drinks a day. Besides, he was under a lot of stress.

Julia padded downstairs in bare feet, wearing black jeans and an oversized lilac shirt. She opened the refrigerator door and bent over the cartons of food, reading their labels. Simon felt a tiny but welcome prickle at the base of his spine. Perhaps he wouldn't be completely without a sex drive for the rest of his life after all.

"How about chicken divan," Julia said, "and this loaf of bread? It smells divine."

"Sure," Simon said. "I can't believe people brought all this stuff over here. It's not like I lost a family member or anything."

"Funeral fairies are dedicated," Julia said. "They are inspired to action by the death of the remotest of acquaintances, casseroles at the ready. Look," she said, turning over the foil container, "this one has the recipe taped to the bottom, just in case you like it so much you want to make it yourself."

While the casserole heated, Julia had a glass of wine and Simon finished his bourbon. He told her about Klett, Mabry, and Morgan's missing notes.

"Morgan without his legal pad is like me without this," Simon said, pulling his narrow reporter's notebook from his jacket pocket, "or you without your PDA. He bought them by the gross and kept one for each project. There should be a pad covered with notes in one of those files on Uwharrie Man. It was just what he did."

"Which means what?" Julia said.

"I think it's possible the murderer nicked them," Simon said, "and that the murder had something to do with Uwharrie Man."

"Wow," Julia said, "that's a stretch if I ever heard one, even for you."

"I know," Simon said, "and Otis doesn't have much sympathy for my idea, plus he forbade me to get involved."

"Wise man," Julia said. "It's much more likely that Morgan was killed for one of the tried and true traditional reasons."

"Money," Simon said. "His sister for her inheritance or a burglar for whatever he could steal. But what worries me is Otis doesn't understand that reputations and publications and honors are the currency of academic careers. I'm going to go over to Morgan's house and systematically search his office for those notes."

"Couldn't they be at work? In the truck? In his briefcase?"

"They're not in the truck, and the police have the briefcase. I doubt they're at work. He had a tiny desk in a shared space, he was on the road all the time, or in the lab. But I'll check."

"Want some help?"

"Yes, thank you, I could use it."

DENISE CAME TO THE door in response to Simon's knock. She wore a black dress and had a pencil stuck behind her ear. She seemed younger than he remembered.

"We're just writing the obituary," she said, leading Simon and Julia into the living room. "This is Linda Lemaire, David's secretary."

"Secretary" understated Mrs. Lemaire's job. Few state employees had their own secretaries. Lemaire worked for the entire archaeology office, answering the phone, managing the office, and doing what word processing the archaeologists couldn't manage themselves. Morgan complained that she spent too much time organizing office parties.

Lemaire, a stocky woman nearing sixty, had dyed red hair shaped and teased in a style that resembled a motorcycle helmet. She wore a black suit and white blouse with wide lace frills that spilled over her collar and poked through the buttons of her suit. Simon introduced both women to Julia. Lemaire handed him a cardboard file box.

"This was all that was in Dr. Morgan's desk drawer at work," Lemaire said. "You know he didn't keep much there. And the police brought back his briefcase. It's in the office already."

"Thanks," Simon said.

Simon and Julia escaped to the office, closing the door behind them.

"Did you see Denise's dress?" Julia whispered to him.

"Yeah, it was black. Otherwise you'd never know she was grieving."

"Raw silk," Julia said. "Ann Taylor, I bet you a thousand dollars. And her shoes were Manolo. Expensive makeup, too."

"She looks better every time I see her," Simon said. "Financial security will do that for a person."

"That Linda woman is the funeral czar, I know it," Julia said. "She'll be running things from now on."

Simon put the box down on the desk and started riffling through it.

"What can I do?" Julia asked.

"Start with 'A' over there in the file cabinets. We're looking for a yellow pad covered with notes about Uwharrie Man or the committee. When I'm done here I'll start with 'Z' and move backwards to meet you."

Julia pulled out the first file drawer. "You think he misfiled his notes? That doesn't seem likely."

"It's not. But I have to make absolutely sure they're not here in the office. First because I promised Mabry and Klett, and second because if they're not here it suggests they were stolen."

Julia didn't say anything.

"Go ahead, say I have a vivid imagination."

"You have a vivid imagination." But she kept searching. Simon didn't want to admit it, but he was glad she was there. Maybe, just maybe, they could revive their love affair. Simon was a one-woman man, and he'd wanted

Julia ever since they'd met standing over a eighty-year-old grave containing an unknown woman's corpse.

Simon quickly went through the file box. It contained several outdated copies of the state employees handbook, a state telephone directory, lots of old memos about parking, health insurance, and such. Also a calculator that didn't work, a few pencils, a box of tissue, and a tin of breath mints. Breath mints? Morgan? Who knew?

Next he turned his attention to the briefcase. If the notes weren't in the files—and Julia appeared to be up to about "C"—they'd most likely be in the briefcase. He opened it. It contained a fresh yellow pad, without any of the pages torn off, a pad of graph paper with an unidentified dig site sketched on it, a zipper bag containing some drawing instruments, a couple of rolls of antacids, two pens and three pencils, and three archaeological journals. The planner was a small cheap date book, with just a few appointments noted on it, of the dentist and poker night sort. The back page had about fifteen names with phone numbers scrawled on it, all of which Simon recognized. The cell phone, which Morgan rarely used, contained no stored numbers. Simon assumed that the police were getting a record of Morgan's recent calls. The police still had Morgan's laptop, too. He usually didn't use it for notes, but he might have drafted an opinion on it.

"Nothing," Simon said, moving to his end of the bank of file cabinets. They worked quickly and quietly, occasionally pulling legal pads out of files and leafing through them. They met in the middle of the "M's." Simon pushed the file drawer shut.

"Well, there are no notes on Uwharrie Man in the file cabinet, the briefcase, the office, or at work," Simon said. "I suppose I should go through the rest of the house in case he set them down somewhere."

He left Julia sitting cross-legged on the floor leafing through the journals from Morgan's briefcase. He went into Morgan's bedroom, where the only paper was between the covers of the Stephen King and Robert B. Parker paperbacks stacked on his nightstand, and the second bedroom, which reminded him of a cheap hotel room.

There were no notes on Uwharrie Man anywhere in the house.

On his way back to the office Denise and Linda waylaid him.

"We need to talk to you about some things," Denise said.

"Of course," Simon said, sitting down on the sofa.

"The obituary will go in the paper tomorrow morning," Linda said. "And the viewing will be tomorrow at the funeral home right before the service."

"Viewing? Do we have to do that?"

"Of course," Denise said. "People will want to pay their last respects. We need to find out from the funeral home if we can have the coffin open."

Simon wished he was sitting on his back porch in the dark with a glass of bourbon listening to an Eric Clapton CD.

"I need you to come to the funeral home with me first thing in the morning," Denise said. "I have an appointment at nine. We need to pick out the coffin and discuss the service. You'll need to write the checks."

Simon felt the muscles of his neck spasm. "Is there time to get everything done?"

"The funeral home assures me the selections will take just a few minutes. The service is already scheduled for the chapel at one in the afternoon. The notice is in today's paper."

This woman wants to get out of Dodge, Simon thought. How hard would it have been to stay just one more day, instead of rushing her brother into his grave?

"Of course," Simon said. "If you need me at the funeral home at nine, I'll be there."

"The pastor from Bloodworth Baptist Church went to the seminary with my pastor, and he's agreed to do the service and preach the eulogy. Then we'll go straight to the cemetery."

Simon thought a memorial service in a secular setting, with a few words from Morgan's friends, would have been more fitting, but he knew he'd lose this battle, so he didn't even try. If Morgan knew, he'd hate it, but he was dead, so what difference did it make? Simon made a mental note to organize a more suitable wake at Players' Retreat later, maybe after Clare came back from Honduras.

"Then we'll have the reception here after the service," Linda said. "I've already got people to organize the food and drink and to decorate the house. They'll be here first thing in the morning."

Simon hoped someone was in charge of alcohol.

"No problem," Denise said. "I'll leave my keys under the doormat when I leave the house."

"Can I read you the obituary?" Denise asked Simon.

"Sure," Simon said. His muscle spasms migrated from his neck to knot between his shoulder blades.

"Here we go," Denise said. "'David Amos Morgan

suddenly joined his heavenly father on Monday, October 10, at his home on Purview Street in Raleigh, North Carolina.' "

Suddenly joined? He was murdered, for God's sake. He didn't just up and decide to board a passing train bound for glory.

" 'David was born in Knoxville, Tennessee, on August 12, 1961. He graduated from high school in Knoxville and attended the University of Tennessee on an ROTC scholarship. After serving four years in the United States Army, he attended graduate school at the University of Oklahoma, receiving his doctorate in archaeology in 1990. Since that time he had been continually employed by the North Carolina Office a State Archaeology. He published numerous articles on the prehistory of North Carolina and was an adjunct professor of prehistory at Kenan College. He is survived by his sister, Denise Morgan McGrath, and three nephews, Henry, Charles, and Earl McGrath, and a special friend, Clare Monahan.' " Denise looked up. "How does this sound so far?" she asked.

Simon's tension had traveled down his spine and back up to encircle his head. He was just plain in pain.

"It's fine," he said.

Denise bent over the paper again.

" 'David was beloved by his family and many friends. Final services will be at Dix Funeral Home at one o'clock P.M. followed by interment in Oakwood Cemetery and a reception at his home.' "

"Don't forget the part about donating to the church in lieu of flowers," Linda said. Must be the price extracted by the preacher for holding a funeral for a stranger.

And Simon wouldn't have said that "beloved" described Morgan. He was a cranky misanthrope most of the time, with just a couple of close friends. His dogs might have loved him. . . .

"Oh, God!" Simon jumped up from the sofa. "The dogs!"

"What?" Denise said. Startled, Linda knocked over her soda.

"I haven't checked on the dogs," Simon said. The one thing Morgan would have really wanted him to do, never mind estates and obituaries, or even finding his killer, was to care for his dogs. And he'd completely forgotten them.

Simon rushed back into Morgan's office in search of his cell phone. Julia still sat on the floor, absorbed in a journal.

"This stuff is fascinating," Julia said. "Did you know that archaeologists can match stone tools to the quarries they came from? And that DNA can be extracted from bone marrow many thousands of years old? And—"

"The dogs," Simon said, "I forgot to check on the dogs." He glanced at his watch, then dialed his voice mail, which he hadn't checked since Morgan's body had been found. He slogged through dozens of voice mails from sympathetic friends until he reached a message from the vet's office.

"Whew," he said, clicking off his phone.

"Are they okay?" Julia asked.

"Yeah, both of them. I can pick them up later tonight. The vet's office is open until ten. God knows what I'll do with them."

He sank down on the floor next to Julia. He leaned his head on her shoulder, and she put her arms around him.

"One day at a time," she said.

"It would be helpful if the days weren't so damn long."

Julia smelled of the scented shampoo she used when she was sharing his bed, and the odor refreshed him. He returned her embrace, circling her waist and pulling her to him, burying his face in her neck. Then he cupped a breast with his hand and kissed her, trying to drown all other feelings except his desire for her.

She put up with his attentions for a few seconds, then pulled away from him.

"Simon—"

"Oh, God, don't start."

"This isn't how I planned to comfort you."

"Julia, how long are we going to keep doing this? It's been years now. We care about each other. Let's do something about it."

Julia ran her fingers through her hair, smoothing it. "If we were just going to be lovers, it would be okay," she said. "But neither of us is getting any younger," she said. "We both want to get married."

"So let's get married," Simon said.

"It wouldn't work," she said. "Not for me."

Simon had always gotten this vibe from Julia. He'd assumed it was his half-Jewish, half-hillbilly background, his height, his lack of financial ambition, but he'd never gotten a full explanation for her on-the-brink-but-not-quite-committed attraction for him.

"Tell me why," he said. "I need to know."

"I can't be your Watson for the rest of my life."

Simon was taken aback.

"Pardon me?" he said. "My what?"

"Your Watson, your assistant."

"That's ridiculous."

"Is it? Then what am I doing here?"

"You offered to help."

"I did. Look, I'm a criminal attorney working for the police department. Your avocation is solving old cold cases. Every time we've been together I've wound up moonlighting as your assistant. It's inevitable. And I'm unhappy about it."

"I'll give it up."

"Baloney. You get too big a rush from solving those old crimes. And you're good at it. Brilliant, actually. But I don't want to play second fiddle to your first violin in a marriage."

Simon knew she was right. He felt strangely flat, almost relieved.

"I think you're okay," she said. "I'm going to go back to your house and get my stuff and go on back to my place tonight."

They both stood up.

"Let me drive you," Simon said.

"I need the walk," she said. " 'Bye."

"Goodbye."

SIMON WAS DESPERATE TO get out of Morgan's house, away from the two women in the front room, but he needed to give Julia half an hour or so to clear out of his house.

He picked up the magazines she'd been reading off the floor and stuffed them back into Morgan's briefcase. His duties as executor suddenly weighed on him. Realistically most of Morgan's possessions that his sister didn't want were destined for the Goodwill store or the dump, but what about his work? It occurred to Simon that he could donate most of it to the Kenan College Library, set up a permanent collection even, with a fund to maintain it. He'd find someone to take over the prehistory course Morgan had taught as an adjunct professor. He had influence in the department—he'd rarely exercised the clout he had as the college's only Pulitzer Prize–winning professor, but he would now. Making this decision, and just maybe finishing with Julia, made him feel infinitely better.

The doorbell rang. Simon looked at his watch. It was late for a social call.

"I'll get it," he called out to Denise. He went to the front door and opened it to a beautiful young woman. She was blond, petite, shapely, and breathless. She wore faded blue jeans, hiking boots, an aqua sweater cut low, an unzipped Carolina sweat jacket, and carried a fashionable tote featuring even more aqua in its print fabric. A gold chain weighed down with several charms hung to her cleavage. Her crimped blond hair swung at her shoulders, bangs ending just at her eyebrows. A Mini Cooper idled in the driveway, the driver's-side door standing open, a Paul Simon song blasting from the CD player.

"I'm Martha Dunn," she said. "I got here as soon as I got Dr. Mabry's message. Am I too late to help?"

6

A baker who vowed to take the recipe for his cinnamon cake to the grave kept his promise by having it etched onto his gravestone. Mourners at the funeral of Jaakov Topor, 93, from Kibbutz Naan in Israel turned up for the funeral to find all the details for his cinnamon cake recipe etched in stone. Topor had kept the recipe secret for more than 75 years.

—*JERUSALEM POST,* JULY 6, 2005

LUKE, THE YOUNGER OF MORGAN'S TWO BLACK LABRADOR retrievers, almost knocked Simon down in the lobby of the vet hospital, he was so grateful to see him. The veterinary assistant who'd brought the dogs from the kennel had to hold the thrashing animal while Simon buckled his collar around his neck and clipped a leash to it. Rex, on the other hand, who had pricked up his ears when entering the lobby, now hung his head down, dejected, his tail sagging between his hind legs. Simon wasn't whom he had expected to see.

"Sorry, boy," Simon said to him, rubbing his ears. "I

wish I could turn the clock back. You're just going to have to settle for me."

"Are you going to keep them?" the vet asked.

Simon was taken aback. He hadn't thought that far ahead. His cats would loathe the dogs, but for now they'd just have to cope.

"I could help you find a home for Luke," the vet said. "I'm afraid Rex is too old to be adoptable. And he seems a bit depressed. If he doesn't perk up in a few days, let me know. There's a good dog antidepressant on the market. And don't forget to give him a buffered aspirin twice a day for his arthritis."

Simon promised to call her if need be.

Simon wedged both dogs into his Thunderbird and drove home, Luke panting wetly in his ear. After his brief conversation with Martha Dunn, he'd packed his car with the dogs' toys, beds, and food so he could take the animals directly to his house. Somehow he felt they shouldn't see their old home again.

He let the dogs out into his fenced back yard. His cats vamoosed through a cat door onto the screened back porch, where they posted themselves on a bench, warily watching the dogs in the yard, tails cricked and jerking.

Simon became a cat person when his ex-wife's cat, Maybelline, whom Tessa had brought to the marriage, refused to leave with her mistress. She'd hidden some-where in the basement until Tessa drove away. Maybelline gave birth to Cecilia and Lucille, and their siblings, before Simon had the sense to get her neutered. He liked the cats. They kept him company and entertained him when he wanted them to, and took care of themselves when he was busy. Dogs were different. They were like people. Needy.

Rex whined at the kitchen door. Simon let him in, and the dog went to his water bowl and slurped messily, splashing water all over the floor. Then he crawled submissively over to Simon and pushed his nose into his hand.

"No need to grovel," Simon said, petting him. He went outside to fetch Luke and found him at the side fence, front paws resting on the top rail, tail wagging furiously, enjoying the attentions of Danny, Simon's teenage neighbor.

"Hey, Simon," Danny said. "I'm really sorry about Dr. Morgan. Man, I was so shocked. How awful. Like, murdered in his own house! Have the police arrested anyone?"

"No," Simon said. "Not yet."

"Can I help you with anything?"

"Actually, you can. I've got Morgan's dogs here. This one's Luke, and the senior citizen inside is Rex. I may be gone a lot in the next few days."

"I'll look after them, I like dogs. Mom's never let me have one. She says we aren't home enough."

Danny's mother worked long hours, so the teenager was often unsupervised. He had never mentioned his father, and Simon didn't ask about him. Simon had spent time with Danny over the years, taking him for batting practice, slipping him spending money in return for his computer expertise, selling him his old Thunderbird. Danny now sported thick dark sideburns, he was nearly six feet tall, and he made his spending money playing the piano all over town. This disconcerted Simon. If Danny was growing older in such a measurable way, Simon must be, too. Lately he'd been checking the crown of his head for thinning hair.

"This guy needs to come inside now," Simon said, grabbing Luke's collar. "I've got to go."

"Let him stay out. I'll play with him for a while," Danny said. "I've still got keys to your house, I'll let him in later."

"Sure," Simon said, "thanks."

"C'mere, dude," Danny said to the dog, opening the gate between his yard and Simon's. "I've got an old tennis ball around here somewhere."

Simon went back inside. Rex lay at the foot of the sofa. He only sighed when he saw Simon, not moving his tail even an inch. Simon wondered how on earth one consoled a grieving dog.

THE NEXT MORNING SIMON parked in the lot behind the Dix Funeral Home. He sat in the car for a few minutes, listening to the radio, collecting himself, furious with Morgan for putting him in this position, furious with himself for being angry with his dead friend. And he was very angry. He actually blamed the man for being up at an uncharacteristic hour in the morning, for working with his back to the unlocked door to his own back yard, for failing to hear his killer creeping up behind him. How dare he deprive Simon of his friendship for the rest of Simon's life and put him through the ordeal of being his executor?

Inside, the funeral home was serene and quiet. A piano piece played softly through concealed speakers in the lobby, decorated tastefully but generically in calm shades of green. Fresh white flowers in cut-glass vases rested on several tables scattered around the room. Two oil paintings, both of ethereal landscapes, one spring and one summer, hung on the wall over a sofa, subliminal reminders of heaven, maybe?

A younger and prettier woman than Simon anticipated came out of an office and greeted him. She was several inches taller than Simon, with long dark brown hair. She wore a black skirt and soft pink cashmere sweater.

"I'm Katie Geil," she said. "Can I help you?"

Simon explained his mission.

"I'm Dr. Morgan's funeral director," she said. "Mrs. McGrath is in our remembrance showroom. We've already completed the paperwork."

"You don't look much like a funeral director," Simon said.

She smiled at him. "Everyone says that," she said. "I think people expect me to wear a black hood and carry a scythe."

The remembrance showroom wasn't what Simon expected, either.

Instead of row upon ominous row of coffins displayed under garish fluorescent lighting, like he'd seen during funeral home scenes in the movies, the space looked more like a home store. Just the corners of coffins, and samples of fittings, jutted out from displays mounted on the walls. Various urns, including some fashioned from porcelain and cloisonné, rested on glass shelves. He rather liked the urn disguised as a short shelf of books. He wondered if a customer could select titles.

Denise stood studying the description of an oak coffin with brass fittings. She wore a trouser suit of heavy linen and carried a leather handbag, one of those stamped with the initials of its designer.

"I think this is nice, don't you?" she asked.

Good morning to you, too, Simon thought.

"Sure," Simon said. He didn't give a damn what coffin

she selected. He just wanted to pay the bill and get the hell out of there.

"Basic vault, I think," Denise said. "The cemetery requires it."

The three of them sat at a round table in a corner to settle the account. The bill, for embalming, coffin, vault, viewing, hosting the funeral service in the chapel, and transportation to and from the cemetery, was $8,897. Simon wouldn't get Morgan's insurance check for two more days, so he handed over his own credit card. He prayed it wouldn't bounce. It didn't.

"Now," the pretty funeral director said, "about the viewing this afternoon. We haven't discussed Dr. Morgan's clothes. We don't have any requirements—these days most people are buried in the clothes they liked to wear in life, even if it's jeans and a polo shirt. We had one man last year who was laid out in his leather motorcycle gear, with his helmet at his side."

"Oh, David must wear a suit," Denise said. "I won't have him buried in those old khakis and boots and flannel shirts of his. He looked like a car mechanic."

"He doesn't, didn't own a suit," Simon said.

"Here," Katie Geil said, handing over her business card. "If you take this to that men's warehouse store on Western Boulevard and give my card to the salesman, they can help you, and they'll give you ten percent off, too. Do you know what sizes your friend wore?"

"Not a clue."

"I'll get his measurements," she said. She went across the hall and through an unmarked door.

Denise looked at her watch. "We need to get to the cemetery and buy the plot," she said.

Katie Geil came back and handed Simon a slip of paper with Morgan's measurements on it, even his shoe size.

The three of them rode to Oakwood Cemetery in one of the funeral home's limousines, where Simon charged $3,800 to his credit card for a nice shady plot overlooking the Confederate section and across a gravel path from the Old Hebrew graveyard. Not a bad price when you thought about it, considering the cemetery promised to mow Morgan's grass for all eternity.

Simon had no idea his credit card could stand this kind of abuse. Once he'd reimbursed himself from Morgan's life insurance, he wondered just how far he could go before he reached the card's limit. He'd always wanted to go to Africa, Botswana especially, and then India and Thailand. He fantasized about selling out, finding a romantically derelict house in Casablanca, lounging around on red leather cushions drinking bourbon all day while feeding dates to a pet monkey, avoiding CNN, love, and life in general, like a character in an Evelyn Waugh novel.

Outside the men's store, Simon leaned his head back on the headrest of his car seat with his eyes closed and took deep diaphragmatic breaths, steeling himself. He wasn't sure what he was trying to control, whether it be laughter, tears, or outrage, but he feared he might break out any moment in what his Aunt Rae would call "inappropriate" behavior. He longed to tear up Morgan's measurements into tiny pieces, toss them in the dumpster in back of the store, set the contents on fire, and dance around it naked. Maybe then his headache would go away.

Inside, he beckoned for a clerk. The nearest salesman,

a soft, middle-aged man with a comb-over, sized him up, brows knitted, wondering how to tell Simon that he was too short to fit at the store. Simon knew and didn't care. He ordered all his clothes from the Lands' End catalog.

"Can I help you?" the salesman asked. "But I'm afraid—"

Wordlessly Simon handed the salesman the funeral director's card.

Immediately the salesman's voice dropped several notches, to a more funereal pitch.

"I am so sorry," he said. "We can take care of everything. What do you need?"

Simon bought a tasteful blue suit, white shirt, and conservative tie. The salesman reminded Simon that he would need suitable underwear, socks, and shoes, and Simon complied. He balked at purchasing a handkerchief that matched the tie.

As the salesman rang up his purchases, Simon noted the size of the black wingtips.

"These are elevens," Simon said. "He wore a twelve."

The salesman laid a reassuring hand on Simon's arm. "We're out of twelves, and the exact size doesn't really matter under the circumstances, does it?" he said.

"Oh, no, of course not," Simon said.

His credit card again rose to the occasion.

Simon tossed his purchases into the passenger seat of his car. Dropping behind the wheel, he collapsed into laughter. He laughed, tears streaming down his face, until his chest ached and he developed hiccups. Imagining his dead friend spending eternity wearing tight wingtips was the funniest thing he'd thought of in days. Finally he was able to stop laughing and start his car.

Simon dropped Morgan's new clothes at the funeral home. He had a couple of errands to run before he went home to change. He hoped the coin shop had the item he wanted.

WHEN SIMON RETURNED HOME he was surprised to see Otis Gates, sitting in his car, smoking a cigarette, waiting for him. He got out of his car when Simon got out of his, crushing his cigarette on the sidewalk with his foot. Otis smoked three cigarettes a day. This was probably his third.

"Hey there," Simon said. "Is this business or social?"

"A little of both," Gates said.

"Come on in," Simon said, opening his door, "have a seat."

Otis waited in the living room while Simon dealt with the animals. He let both dogs out, then back in, and fed them. He took food and water to his cats, still languishing in purgatory on the screened porch. Before he went into the living room he poured himself a bourbon, disguising it by filling the rest of the glass with Coke.

"These are Morgan's dogs?" Otis asked, when Simon finally sat down across from him in his father's leather Mission armchair. "I'm glad they survived."

"Me, too," Simon said. "I think eventually I'll look for a new home for the young one, but I may need to keep Rex myself. He's getting up there."

Otis crossed his legs and leaned back into the sofa, fiddling with his notebook.

"We got the dogs' blood work back. They were sedated with diphedryl. A common antihistamine. It's available over the counter in allergy tablets and sleeping aids."

"So anyone could get it. How long until it would take effect?"

"As much as they had, maybe half an hour. They'd be out cold. But the problem is, this doesn't help us decide if the murder was premeditated. Lots of people carry these pills around. Morgan's killer could have given the medication to the dogs in advance, like we supposed—"

"Or he could have slipped it to the dogs on the spur of the moment—"

"Or even after the crime, to disguise the fact that the dogs knew him. But there's more. Denise McGrath doesn't have an alibi."

"You're kidding."

"No. She wasn't at home, she said she was at a teachers' conference in Nashville, and she registered for the conference, but she didn't pick up her badge or stay at the hotel."

Simon didn't know what to say. He didn't much like Denise McGrath, but she was Morgan's sister, for God's sake.

Gates took out a pack of cigarettes, then put it back in his pocket. Looking for something for his hands to do, he flipped through the pages of his notebook without looking at them.

"I like the sister for it," he said, "I can't deny that. She could have skipped the conference, driven up here, killed her brother, and gone home."

"About the Uwharrie Man committee, Otis, I—"

"I didn't ignore your suggestions, Simon. I checked on the alibis of the members of the committee. None of them have a story that can be verified. Klett says he was at home, but he and his wife sleep in separate bedrooms because he snores. Mabry is divorced and lives alone. Lowery lives in Pembroke, but he spent the night, alone, at a hotel here in town because a committee meeting had been scheduled for the next day. Ms. Lambert keeps a studio apartment here, but she goes home on the weekend to her home on the Cherokee reservation, where her husband manages the craft cooperative. She was sleeping at her apartment alone at the time of the murder. No one has a good alibi for five o'clock in the morning."

"I suppose you've fingerprinted them?"

"Yeah, but the committee met once at Morgan's house, a couple of weeks ago. Klett said he and Morgan hoped a neutral environment would calm everyone down."

"So it would mean nothing if you found their finger-prints in the house."

"Given your friend's housekeeping habits, yeah. By the way, what do you know about Mabry's graduate student, Martha Dunn? What stake does she have in all this?"

"If Uwharrie Man is returned to the Lumbee, her doc-toral thesis turns to dust overnight."

Gates smiled, for the first time since he'd come in the house. "Let me write that down. That's good. Have you met Brad Lowery?"

"Not yet. But any one of the committee members had opportunity."

"You've got academic infighting over a bunch of bones, a missing legal pad, folks who don't have an alibi at a time of day that most people don't. It's just not as compelling a motive as four hundred thousand dollars. Mrs. McGrath is at the top of my list. Why would a woman like her fake attending a teachers' conference and vanish for two days?

And no matter how common these antihistamines are, sedating the dogs still speaks of premeditation to me."

"What does Denise say?"

"She insists she was at the conference, the hotel's lost her records, there was a badge mix-up, maybe there were two badges with her name, that kind of thing. I'm questioning her again today."

"Why are you telling me all this? I thought I was supposed to stay out of this case."

Gates sighed heavily. "You were, you still are, but I need your help."

Simon bit his tongue.

"I'll do whatever I can," he said.

"Our computer guys have been going through Dr. Morgan's laptop. There's nothing much there. A few e-mails, a number of documents, articles, a couple of Internet searches . . ."

"Uwharrie Man?"

"Not a word about the committee's work. But would you look through the material and see if anything jumps out at you?"

"Of course," Simon said, reaching for the CD Gates held out to him.

"Everything's downloaded onto this," Gates said. "We've got another one at the station." Gates stuck his notebook back in his jacket pocket.

"I'd offer to buy you lunch," Simon said, "but I've got to dress for the funeral."

"I'll see you there," Gates said.

———

THE DOGS CROWDED AROUND Simon's legs, craving his attention, trying to distract him from dressing. He'd showered, shaved, found a clean, respectable shirt with a collar, and pressed the wrinkles out of the dark suit he kept for such occasions. Downstairs in the kitchen he tried to eat some cheese and crackers, gave up, and fed them to the dogs. Morgan's viewing was only half an hour or so away. Standing around someone's corpse didn't appeal to him at all, but he knew it was important to Denise and he didn't want to display a lack of respect. He wondered about Denise McGrath. Could she really have killed her brother?

He thought about the option he and Otis hadn't discussed, the easy scenario, the stranger murder, which criminologists said rarely happened. Some down-and-out at the liquor store saw the wad of money Morgan carried in his wallet and followed him home. He came back in the early morning with doctored treats for the dogs, waited for them to fall asleep, broke into the house, surprised Morgan, and killed him. He stole the cash in Morgan's wallet, his watch, and a few artifacts from a shelf, hoping they were valuable, and took off. But if that were the truth, Denise McGrath should be able to prove she was at her conference, and Simon should have found Morgan's notes.

His telephone rang. Reaching for the receiver, he saw his uncle's New York City number on the caller ID.

"Hi, Morris," Simon said.

"Hello yourself," Morris Simon answered. "You wonder why I'm calling, I bet."

Simon racked his brains. Usually he and his New York

family talked on a regular schedule, every two weeks on a Sunday afternoon, unless it was a Jewish holiday.

"Of course I know," Simon said. "It's Erev Yom Kippur."

"You remembered, I'm proud," his uncle said. "I was going to remind you to pray."

"I'll be praying, I promise," Simon said. He wondered where his prayer book was. He'd promised his uncle when he'd last seen him that he'd work at practicing his mother's religion.

"Have you done the required mitzvahs?"

"Absolutely." If taking care of Morgan's estate wasn't a mitzvah, he didn't know what was.

"So how are you?"

"Fine," Simon said, "just fine." He didn't tell his uncle about the murder, he just didn't have the energy. He'd e-mail him later with the whole story, including, he hoped, who the murderer was. After he hung up, he resolved again to keep his promise and say the appropriate ancient prayers before he went to bed tonight. It couldn't hurt. The Shema had sustained his mother's people through a lot of troubles far worse than one man's murder.

THE MOOD IN THE lobby of the funeral home was somber and respectful. There was a grandmotherly sort manning the reception desk and a couple of men in blue suits standing around the lobby. If they'd been wearing dark glasses they would have looked like FBI agents. One of them leaned toward Simon, speaking in such a quiet voice Simon had to strain to hear him.

"May I ask whom you are visiting this afternoon?" he asked.

"Dr. David Morgan," Simon said.

"Right over there," the man said, gesturing toward a doorway at the end of the hall. "The end of the hall, to your right."

Simon was very early. The room was empty except for the coffin resting in the middle of the room on a raised platform, flanked with two tall candlesticks. The candles were lit, and the coffin was open. He paced the border of the room a couple of times, building up his resolve. Oh, damn it to hell, Simon thought. He fumbled in his pocket for the items he'd brought with him, and made his way over to the coffin. Inside it, resting his head on a silk cushion, hands clasped over his chest, was a man Simon had never seen before. Simon was in the wrong damn room. He'd have to go through this all over again.

Out in the hall he ran into Katie Geil.

"You're early," she said. "Dr. Morgan's viewing doesn't start for fifteen minutes. His sister's not here yet."

"I know," Simon said. "Igor over there sent me to the wrong room."

Katie hid her smile behind a hand.

"Oh, Dr. Shaw! That is Dr. Morgan, I promise! You'd be surprised how often people don't recognize the deceased."

Simon went back into the room and gave the corpse another look. It was Morgan, all right, but disguised as a banker.

"You look better than you ever did alive," Simon said to him. Morgan was neatly dressed in the suit Simon had bought, but what had fooled him was the short-back-and-sides haircut, which must have been at Denise's request.

"Sorry about the shoes," Simon said, then had to suppress breaking out into uncontrolled laughter. He heard the sound of Denise's voice behind him, so he quickly slipped the items he'd brought under Morgan's pillow, a cigarette, the latest Stephen King paperback, a rock pick, and a coin, a genuine drachma he'd purchased that afternoon, for the ferryman.

Simon endured the next thirty minutes as best he could chatting with Denise and Linda, neither of whom ventured near the coffin. After enough people arrived to keep Denise occupied, he escaped to the chapel to wait for the funeral to begin.

7

I am ready to meet my Maker. Whether my Maker is ready
to meet me is another matter.

—WINSTON CHURCHILL ON HIS SEVENTY-FIFTH BIRTHDAY

SIMON HAD WONDERED HOW MANY MOURNERS WOULD BE AT
Morgan's funeral service. He was glad to see a respectable
assortment of friends, neighbors, and coworkers, enough
to nearly fill the funeral home chapel. Walker Jones and
Sophie Berelman represented the Kenan College history
department, which Morgan had served as an adjunct professor, but they were there for Simon's sake, too, and he
was grateful to them for coming. He slid into the pew
behind them. Walker grasped his hand, and Sophie
hugged him. Marcus Clegg and his daughter, Trina, Morgan's protégée, if a man could be said to have a preteen
protégée, sat across the aisle. Trina, who was, charitably
speaking, going through an ugly duckling phase, looked
rumpled and ill at ease in a new dress and black flats. A
cowlick that had rippled through her brown hair since
birth still wasn't controlled. She kicked the pew in front of

her until Marcus stopped her, then crossed her arms and sulked.

Simon knew from experience how difficult it was to be a brilliant child. Everyone thought of you as a nerd in training. If Simon hadn't lettered in baseball in high school, he would never have had a social life. And Trina had girl issues. Julia once carefully explained to him why Trina's three blond sisters were such a heavy burden for her to carry.

Simon leaned back in the pew and cased the crowd. Denise McGrath and Linda Lemaire sat in the front pew, as befitted the deceased's next of kin and the funeral czar. Henry Klett and a sweet-looking woman Simon assumed was his wife sat across the aisle with Lawrence Mabry and Martha Dunn. A few rows farther back sat Brenda Lambert and Brad Lowery, whom he recognized from their résumé photographs in Morgan's files. Lowery fidgeted constantly, crossing and uncrossing his legs, straightening his collar and jacket, folding and unfolding the bulletin. At the last minute Otis Gates slid into the pew next to Simon, nodding at him before he pulled his notebook and pencil from his jacket pocket. It might be an urban legend that many murderers attended their victims' funerals, but Gates took no chances. He'd take note of everyone at the service, and ask the names of those he didn't recognize. Simon doubted he'd show up at the reception. Might affect the conversation. Instead he'd pester Simon for details of what went on there.

The service lasted just twenty minutes, but it seemed interminable to Simon. It was generic, not personal to Morgan at all. The musical selections were predictable and the scripture readings even more so. The eulogy had to be canned. The minister just filled Morgan's name in the blanks. Finally the service ended, and the mourners escaped into the crisp autumn air to drive to the cemetery. The cars formed an old-fashioned funeral procession, driving thirty miles an hour with their headlights on. Pedestrians on the sidewalks along the way automatically bowed their heads.

The grave-side ceremony was more bearable for Simon. He liked the Christian interment ceremony. The ashes to ashes and dust to dust imagery appealed to him, and so did the expressed hope in resurrection. It gave an optimistic touch to the otherwise gloomy proceedings. After the interment liturgy the minister offered the mourners a chance to drop flowers on the coffin. Many did, including Simon. Trina was the last to participate. She threw her lily down angrily and turned back to her father, throwing herself into his arms. Marcus held her to him as they walked to their car. Simon hadn't yet seen her cry.

LINDA LEMAIRE AND HER funeral fairies had transformed Morgan's house. They couldn't disguise the dingy walls and eighties decor, but they'd waxed the hardwood floors, tossed ready-made slipcovers over the battered furniture, and placed vases of fresh flowers all around the living room. Two portable tables draped with starched, embroidered linen cloths groaned under the weight of platters of funeral food and beer and wine. Another table displayed photographs of Morgan—at a dig, giving a lecture, in his lab—and a remembrance book for the mourners to sign. Trina carefully wrote a long entry in it, while her father stood behind her with his hands on her shoulders. Then without a word she went straight to the buffet table and stacked her plate with cake, brownies, and cookies. Her father made no attempt to moderate her selections, or to remind her to be polite. She went out onto the back patio, despite the chill, to eat alone.

"How is she doing?" Simon asked Marcus.

"Not very well," Marcus said. "She won't talk about him at all. Just hangs around the house moping, picking fights with her sisters. And she was driving us crazy before Dr. Morgan died. Marianne says just to leave her be. We've dealt with one issue, though."

"What?"

"We've managed to give her a bedroom of her own. We moved the washer and dryer out of the utility room into the garage. I built a loft bed in the utility room over the weekend. The family computer is still a bone of contention, though. We've put her on a strict schedule so the others get a chance to use it. Recently I've felt more like a policeman than a father."

Now that the funeral was over Simon felt his stress wane a bit. He was still terribly sad, but he felt the worst was over. He got a beer and loaded a plate with ham, chicken salad, sweet potato casserole—with marshmallows—buttered yeast rolls, and cake. He didn't forget that one of his priorities was to meet Brad Lowery. Lowery stood with Brenda Lambert, so he went over to them and introduced himself. They couldn't shake hands because of their food and drink, so the three of them just nodded at each other. Lowery didn't waste time getting down to business.

"Henry Klett told me you were looking for Dr. Morgan's notes," he said. "Have you found them yet?"

Lowery looked much as he had when Simon saw him on television. He was stocky, in his late thirties, with dark brown hair and blue eyes, not uncommon for a Lumbee Indian. He wore a blue suit, white shirt, and a bolero tie with a hammered silver clasp.

"Let me say, on behalf of the Native American community, first," Lambert said, "how sorry we are about Dr. Morgan's death. He was a pleasure to work with." Lambert was a small, middle-aged, solidly built woman. Her black hair, pulled back in a bun, was thickly striped with gray and she wore a gray flannel coatdress with a silver and beadwork eagle brooch pinned to one lapel.

"He listened," Lowery said. "I respected him for that."

"Thank you," Simon said. "And no, I haven't found his notes. There's nothing on his computer about the Uwharrie Man committee, either, although he'd been researching the issues involved on the Internet."

"How odd," Lambert said. "We saw him taking notes. Pages of them. What do you think happened to them? They didn't just vanish into thin air."

"It doesn't matter now," Lowery said. "The governor will have to appoint a new committee."

"Unless we can compromise," Lambert said.

Lowery hooted. "Professor Lawrence Mabry will settle for no less than picking at our ancestor's bones like a vulture," he said, "and then tastefully displaying them for white schoolchildren to gawk at, like his kind have been doing to our dead for generations."

"Native Americans and anthropologists have managed to work together to study our history all over the country," Lambert said. "There's no reason why we can't do the same here in North Carolina. You and Mabry are each going to have to give a little." Lambert turned to Simon.

"Your friend Dr. Morgan felt we could reach a compromise," she said. "He didn't believe that science and religion are mutually exclusive."

That was news to Simon. "He told you that?" Simon said. "I didn't know he had a religious bone in his body."

"I don't know about that," Lowery said. "But he respected our opinion. Those people," he said, nodding across the room at Klett, Mabry, and Martha Dunn, "science is their god. They think our culture and religion belong in a glass case in a museum."

Lowery drained the last inch of beer in his glass and drifted off toward the food.

"You know," Lambert said, "Dr. Morgan and I were supposed to meet prior to the committee meeting the day he died. We were going to discuss some of the compromises made between archaeologists and other Indian tribes in hopes we could work something out." She displayed the calm of a longtime civil servant used to political storms whipping up and blowing over.

"Really," Simon said.

"You don't think," she said, "that Dr. Morgan's murder could have something to do with Uwharrie Man? It's a contentious issue, but murder? That would mean"—she glanced around the room—"that one of the committee members killed him? I don't believe it."

"The police don't think so, either," Simon said.

SIMON WANDERED INTO THE kitchen, looking for a place to leave his dirty plate, and found Julia arranging pimiento cheese sandwiches on a platter. She wasn't at the funeral;

she must have been here helping to set up for the reception. He felt a pang of regret when he saw her.

"Don't look so surprised to see me," she said, pecking Simon on the cheek. "He was my friend, too."

Simon slipped a sandwich off the tray.

"You look a little better," she said to him.

"I dreaded the funeral most of all," Simon said. "It was so what he wouldn't have wanted. Settling the estate will be a snap compared to sitting through that service."

Julia lowered her voice to a whisper. "Have you seen what Denise McGrath is wearing?" she asked.

"Something black?"

"It's a St. John suit. And she's carrying a Kate Spade bag. She's been to Saks."

"Why not? She's come into money."

"She's gotten her hair cut by a real pro, too. David Wade, I'll bet."

If Denise was guilty of murdering her brother, Simon wondered, would she be so quick to spend his money? Wouldn't she be pretending to express a little more grief?

Martha Dunn came into the kitchen, on the same quest as Simon. She put down her dishes in the soapy water of the sink, leaving them for someone else to wash, and hooked an arm in Simon's.

"Where are we going to eat tonight?" she asked him.

Julia raised an eyebrow.

"You decide," Simon said. "Anywhere is fine with me. I'll pick you up at seven."

"Okay," she said. "I'll be ready. I'll see you then. I'm off to the library for the rest of the afternoon."

After she'd left, Julia snickered at him. "You work

fast," she said. "Aren't there rules about professors dating undergraduates?"

"She's a graduate student," Simon said. "At Carolina. Mabry's her thesis advisor."

"Her skirt's a little short for a funeral, don't you think?"

"Didn't notice. And it's not a date. She came over to the house last night after you left. Since she was too late to help search the office, we arranged to have dinner. I'm going to pump her about the committee. She's been carrying water for Lawrence Mabry for years."

THE CROWD THINNED, BUT Simon felt it was his duty to stay to the bitter end. Trina waved to him as she and her father left. Both Sophie and Walker found him to shake his hand before leaving.

"I'll be at work tomorrow," Simon said.

"There's no need," Walker said. "Wait until Monday."

"I'd rather come on in," Simon said. He didn't want to spend the day watching Denise pack.

As far as Simon could tell, Mabry and Lowery had never spoken, never even nodded at each other. Klett and Lambert had spent a few minutes together, and each had spoken to Mabry and Lowery separately. Mabry and Lowery must despise each other. If they couldn't speak, how could the committee ever reach a compromise? Simon reminded himself to tell Otis.

As the funeral reception broke up, Simon went looking for Denise McGrath. He found her in Morgan's bedroom, lying on his bed on her back, one arm flung across her eyes.

"That's over," Simon said, sitting on the end of the bed.

"Thank God," she said, sitting up.

"Don't get up," he said. "You must be worn out."

"No more than you," she said.

She put her hand out to him. Surprised, he took it, and she squeezed it.

"I want you to know how grateful I am for everything you've done. I'm not usually, well, this hard. It's just that David's death on top of my husband's accident, and the money . . ." Tears began to flow down her cheeks. She pulled tissue out of her designer purse. Simon felt his own eyes sting. Denise sopped up her tears, removing gobs of makeup as she did.

"You've probably heard that Sergeant Gates hasn't found evidence that I was at the teachers' conference. That's just nuts. I've got my receipts and conference materials and everything at home. Once I get there I'll straighten everything out. I promise you I didn't kill my brother."

"I believe you," Simon said. He did, too.

BACK HOME SIMON LET the dogs out. He lived in an old house, and his only good shower was downstairs, near the kitchen where the water pressure was more than a trickle. He stripped and got in the shower with an ice-cold Coke spiked with Goody's headache powders. He let the water run as hot as he could bear it. He left the door to the bathroom open so he could hear the dogs. When Rex scratched at the door, he got out of the shower, wrapped a towel around himself, and let him in.

"If you were a cat," Simon said to him, "you'd have come in yourself through the cat door, and I'd still be in the shower."

Simon never napped, but today was an exception.

Upstairs he collapsed across his bed, just to rest his eyes, and fell asleep. He woke up an hour later with a start, after wondering in his sleep where the other dog was. He pulled on jeans and a sweatshirt and ran downstairs and out into his back yard. No Luke. He called for him, and had just begun to panic when Danny came out his back door with the dog.

"Sorry, Simon," Danny said. "I was playing with him, and then I had to go do my homework, and he wanted to come inside with me. I lost track of the time."

"It's okay," Simon said.

"How was the funeral?"

"It was a funeral." He noticed Luke rubbing up against Danny's leg while the boy's hand stroked his head. His eyes met Danny's.

"Mom says I can have him," Danny said. "I'll take good care of him, I swear. And when I go to college Mom says she'd like the company. And Rex can visit him."

"He's yours," Simon said.

"Yes!" Danny said. The dog, sensing Danny's elation, began to bark and leap. "Thank you!"

"You're welcome."

Simon went back inside. Rex lay on the living room floor. Simon wondered when he should call the vet about the old dog's depression. Now that Luke was gone, his cats would probably venture back inside. Rex wouldn't bother them. Maybe he'd even enjoy the company.

Simon had some time to spare before he picked up Martha, so he took the CD Gates had given him up to his study, a small room with three walls lined with packed bookshelves, his desk facing out of the one window down the alley behind his house. A neighbor had turned on the fairy lights he'd draped through all the trees in his back yard. A car slowly came down the alley, rumbling over cobblestones before turning onto the main street. A dog followed, just a shadow in the shade under the trees, sniffing garbage cans, foiled by the huge green bins dispensed by the city last year. Rex followed him upstairs, curled up at his feet, and began to snore. Simon turned on his laptop and slipped the CD Gates had given him into the port.

Morgan was not a member of the digital generation. His computer was a tool, like his picks and brushes, nothing else. The contents of his e-mail and documents folders were sparse and impersonal. With his penchant for paper and file cabinets, he would have printed out most of what he wanted to keep and filed it away. Simon found a few draft memos and reports in the documents file, but nothing relating to Uwharrie Man. He'd bookmarked just his bank, Clare's church, the state employees Web site, and the Office of State Archaeology's Web site.

Until recently, when Morgan visited and bookmarked dozens of Web sites. Simon went through them. They had pretentious titles like "Ore Petrography and Archaeological Provenance," "Pre-Columbian trans-oceanic contact," "A Review of the Hypotheses and Evidence Relating to the Origins of the First Americans," "The Antiquity of Humankind in the Americans," "Did Aussies Get Here First?" "The Solutrean," and more. Morgan had been an expert on the Woodland culture in the Southeast. These sites were related to Uwharrie Man and the antiquity of humankind in the New World, and so to Morgan's work on the committee. That was clear.

Simon checked the time stamps on the bookmarks. Most of them had been saved the day of Morgan's murder, starting after midnight and continuing into the wee hours. Morgan hadn't woken up early on the morning of his murder. He'd been up all night when he was surprised by his killer.

SIMON CHANGED INTO GRAY slacks and a black leather coat for his date—no, he told himself, his appointment—with Martha Dunn. Simon wondered if she had a boyfriend, and if being gorgeous had a positive or negative effect on an academic career. If she was successful, would people wonder if her looks helped her along the way? Or would they distract her colleagues to the point that she lost opportunities? Looks could affect men's careers, too, but only at the extreme ends of the spectrum, Brad Pitt handsome or bucktoothed ugliness.

Martha sat on a bench outside her apartment complex waiting for him. He pulled into the parking space nearest her and got out.

"Am I late?" he asked.

"Not at all," she said. "I didn't want you to have to wander all over the building looking for my apartment."

She stood up, and Simon had that rare feeling he got when he was taller than a woman. He was a small man, but not often self-conscious about it. His ex-wife was almost exactly his height. Julia was several inches taller. Looking down at Martha aroused a manly, dominating, definitely sexual feeling that was silly, but real nonetheless.

Martha was even prettier than the last time he'd seen her. A rhinestone clip held a lock of shiny blond hair behind one perfect ear. Clear blue eyes loomed large in her heart-shaped face. Her black sheath dress was cut low enough over her breasts and high enough above her knees to be stimulating without being gratuitous. Despite the slight chill in the October air, her legs were bare and tan. She carried a lightweight sweater and a silver handbag.

Simon opened the car door for her.

"I'm surprised you live here and not in Chapel Hill," he said.

"It's closer to the museum. I expected to spend most of my time there while I was writing my dissertation."

"Uwharrie Man?"

"Yes, unfortunately."

"I'm so sorry. How far along are you in the process?"

"I've passed my orals and writtens, and submitted the proposal and literature review. When the legal wrangling over the bones began I postponed everything else. I still get a stipend as Dr. Mabry's research assistant, and I teach a couple of courses at State on my own while I wait."

Condemned to adjunct assistant professor hell.

"What are you going to do?"

"If Uwharrie Man is buried by the Lumbee and I can't finish my thesis? I don't want to think about it. I'm not sure I have the energy to start the process again."

THE HOSTESS AT IRREGARDLESS Café, picked up two menus and led them through the restaurant.

"Your usual table?" she asked Simon.

"Please," Simon said.

"What's good tonight?" Martha asked.

"Everything, of course," the hostess said.

When their waitress arrived, they decided to split a smoked shrimp pizza appetizer and follow it with filet mignons with Madeira peppercorn sauce. They agreed on a bottle of pinot noir.

Martha had, without realizing it, passed a test. She ate red meat.

"This" Martha said, after the waitress moved away, "is a pleasant place to hold an interrogation."

"How transparent am I?"

"Very. But I have questions for you, too."

Their appetizer and wine arrived. Both were wonderful. Simon decided to lay his cards on the table.

"I want to know about your boss, Lawrence Mabry."

"Why?"

"I can't stop wondering if Morgan's murder had something to do with the work of the committee charged with deciding the fate of Uwharrie Man."

She put her wineglass on the table and frowned, wrinkling her forehead. "You think a member of the committee murdered Dr. Morgan? That's a serious accusation."

"I know. But I think I have a responsibility to make it. No one else is, certainly not the police. Your turn to ask a question."

"I'm wondering if you have Dr. Morgan's notes and aren't releasing them. Or I should say, Dr. Mabry wonders, and probably Dr. Klett and Brad Lowery wonder the same thing."

Simon was taken aback.

"Why would I do such a thing?"

"Because you have your own agenda. You disagree with his opinion, so you've hidden the notes, or destroyed them, so as to influence the outcome."

"Whoa," Simon said. "That's a stretch."

"Academics can be a vicious occupation."

Simon refilled their wineglasses.

"I don't have his notes," he said.

"You can see why that would look suspicious," she said. "I mean, where could they be?"

"My theory is the murderer took them."

"Let's look at it this way," she said. "If he was murdered by, say, his sister for his money—"

"How did you hear about that?"

"It's common sense. Money's often the motive for murder, isn't it? As I was saying, say his sister killed him, it had nothing to do with the committee, but his notes are missing. You are the obvious person to have taken them, for some nefarious purpose of your own."

"I didn't take them. I don't give a rat's ass about Uwharrie Man. Not compared to finding Morgan's murderer, anyway."

"What do the police think?"

"I don't know, and I couldn't tell you if I did."

"Stalemate," she said.

Their food arrived, and they ate with gusto. After they were finished they ordered coffee, liqueur, and raspberry chocolate cake. Martha passed another test. She ordered her own dessert instead of eating half of his.

They had more coffee.

"You asked about Dr. Mabry," she said. "I've been working with him now for several years. What do you know about him? Can I trust you not to repeat anything I say?"

"Yes, absolutely," Simon said. "I've seen his résumé, he seems like the worst kind of celebrity professor to me. I think it's the black clothes and contact lenses. Am I being unfair?"

"No," she said, "and his résumé doesn't bear close scrutiny."

"Padded?"

"Most of it's true. His work at Hardaway, for example.

He dug there first as an undergraduate at Chapel Hill and then off and on throughout his career. He wrote his dissertation on whether the Hardaway assemblage represented early Clovis or a pre-Clovis culture—he concluded for the latter. He spent several years in France, where he studied the Solutrean, at the Solutré Cave in Saône-et-Loire. He's consulted at Topper, in South Carolina, and Cactus Hill, in Virginia, both unverified but promising pre-Clovis sites. He's an expert."

"But?"

"There's a lot of other nonsense, claims, on his résumé that just aren't true. Like, where he says he served in Vietnam he was actually in the Reserve and spent his time on active duty writing press releases at Fort Bragg."

"Has he ever taken credit for your work?"

Martha finished the last bite of her dessert.

"You do have a blunt way about you," she said. "He's come this close," she said, holding her thumb and forefinger about a quarter inch apart, "but not so close that I could complain."

Simon wanted to know if Mabry had ever made a pass at her, and if she'd ever capitulated, but his raising by decent folk prevented him from asking.

"I have zero tolerance for résumé exaggeration," Simon said, "and for academic puffery in general. Some say that's why I'm not at a major university."

"I wondered about that."

"It's simple; I want to teach undergraduates. Nothing else interests me as much."

"Dr. Mabry hasn't so much as crossed paths with an undergraduate in years."

A crowd of hungry diners waited at the entrance to the restaurant for a table.

"We should go," Simon said. "Let them turn over this table. It's early—if you like, we could go back to my place for a bit. Have another coffee."

"I'd love to."

SIMON BROUGHT A TRAY with coffee and cups, cream and sugar, into the living room and set it on the coffee table.

"I've got some coffee liqueur friends brought me from Costa Rica," he said. "Want some?"

"Absolutely."

Simon brought in the bottle.

"Just pour it right in there," she said, pointing at her cup.

He poured a generous amount into both cups.

Martha leaned over to pet Rex, who lay at their feet.

"Is this your dog? He's really old, isn't he?"

"He's Morgan's dog—mine now, I suppose. He's not as old as all that. He's quite depressed, I'm afraid."

"Poor thing," she said, rubbing him behind the ears. Rex's tail moved infinitesimally.

"The vet said to call her if he didn't perk up. Apparently even dogs can get antidepressants these days."

Martha sat back up and sipped from her cup.

"You said something in the restaurant," Simon said, "that I'm just now digesting. Does Mabry really think I'm concealing Morgan's notes?"

"Yes," she said, "he does."

"Interesting."

"They can't just have vanished."

"No."

"Couldn't he have left them somewhere?"

"Possible, but I think they would have been returned by now."

Warmed by alcohol, released from his preoccupation with Julia, relieved that his friend's funeral was over, Simon did something he would kick himself over for days afterward. He moved onto the sofa next to Martha and took her hand. She put her cup down on the coffee table and turned to him, giving him permission with her smile.

SIMON KISSED HER GENTLY, and when she responded, he shifted into fourth gear, skipping second and third entirely. Within seconds she was on his lap. He kissed her passionately, starting with her lips and moving south, while she grabbed his hand and moved it under her skirt and upward. She was willing and eager, so he led her upstairs to his bedroom, where they made love, twice, scattering their clothes, tangling the bedcovers, abandoning any reserve you'd think two people who'd met after spending part of the day at a funeral would have.

Simon congratulated himself on his work. Martha fell asleep, curled up naked in his arms. He reached up, turned off his bedside light, which they had both wanted on during lovemaking, pulled the covers up over them both, and followed her into deep sleep.

8

Either that wallpaper goes, or I do.

—OSCAR WILDE (1854–1900),

SPOKEN AS HE LAY DYING IN A DRAB PARIS HOTEL BEDROOM

MARTHA LAY CURLED UP NEXT TO HIM IN HIS BED, BLOND hair tousled, an arm thrown across his chest. He lifted the bedclothes to look at her. She was still naked and as lovely as he remembered. He pulled the covers back up, tucked them gently around her, and rolled out of bed as quietly as he could. It was early, not yet seven. He threw on a bathrobe and went downstairs, let Rex outside, brewed a pot of coffee, and climbed into the shower.

He supposed he shouldn't have slept with Martha, but they'd had a fine dinner and good conversation that led to great lovemaking. It was consensual, and it was fun, even if his conscience reminded him that Julia had just dumped him and he'd buried his best friend yesterday, and he might not be in the best emotional state to make decisions. Then there were the ulterior motives they'd each had for going out together in the first place. He quizzed her about Lawrence Mabry and the Uwharrie Man committee, she wanted to know if he had any information about Morgan's intended vote. Martha had as potent an interest in the outcome of the committee's work as anyone else. Finishing her thesis depended on the committee deciding to allow Lawrence Mabry to analyze Uwharrie Man's bones and the artifacts found with him.

Frankly, right now he didn't give a damn about any of that.

Last night just felt too good.

He'd gotten out of the shower, pulled on some clothes, and let Rex in and fed him when he heard Martha clattering down the stairs. She ran into the kitchen wearing only panties and one of his sweatshirts and jumped into his arms, wrapping her bare legs around his waist.

"I had so much fun last night!" she said.

"Me, too," Simon said, holding her tightly and kissing her.

She slipped out of his arms.

"It came as a surprise to me," she said. "I didn't plan it."

"Neither did I."

"I'd rather stay right here in your bed for the next week or so, but I've got to be standing in front of my Archaeology Intro class in an hour," she said, "and I haven't got any work clothes with me!"

"I've got to get to work, too. I'll pour some coffee, you go cover up that sweet little bum, and I'll drive you back to your place."

"Usually I get up early and go to the waffle house to prep before class, but this time I'll just have to wing it. Hope the glow isn't obvious."

She hurried back up the stairs.

"MAKE YOURSELF AT HOME while I take my shower," Martha said.

"Babe, I should go on to my office."

"Please stay. I want another kiss before I leave. What are you doing tonight?"

"Spending it with you."

Martha went back into her bedroom to shower and change. Simon sank onto her sofa. Martha had good taste. Her small apartment contained some nice pieces of furniture, a camelback sofa, a coffee table, a mahogany server, and a vintage armchair upholstered in silk. Two oil paintings in antique frames hung on the wall over the sofa. An ancient television coated with dust sat on an carved wooden African stool in a corner. The requisite photographs and some good porcelain crowded the top of the coffee table.

The dining nook next to her tiny kitchen served as Martha's office. She'd set up a portable table and stacked it with books, papers, a laptop computer, and a printer. Behind that, on a wall, was a bookcase crowded with books, files, and mementos.

Simon inhaled sharply and felt his blood pressure rise, sending blood pulsing in his head. For a second his heart paused, and when it restarted he thought it would pound its way out of his chest. He went over to the bookshelf behind the makeshift desk. Two pots, a stone pipe, and a Folsom spear point, part of Morgan's stolen collection, rested on one shelf of the bookcase.

Simon couldn't believe it. He forced himself to calm down and think. He examined the objects closely, even picking up the Folsom point. His hand actually trembled. Could he really say these were some of the items missing from Morgan's office? There must be hundreds of similar artifacts in private collections all over the state. As long as they weren't found on state property there wasn't any law against keeping or selling them. Surely Martha wouldn't have invited him here if she had items stolen from Morgan's office on display. He put the point back on the bookshelf. No, he couldn't identify these as Morgan's. He must be emotionally more disjointed than he realized for it even to occur to him.

Martha came out of her bedroom dressed in jeans, a low-cut blue sweater, and clogs, straight into his arms. He pulled the entire length of her body to him and kissed her hard.

"It's funny how things work out, isn't it?" she said, after pulling away from him to catch her breath. "We would never have met if your friend hadn't died."

Simon's gut roiled. "Yeah," he said, "funny."

As casually as he could manage, he nodded at the artifacts. "Those are interesting," he said. "Where did you get them?"

"Flea market," she said. "I shouldn't have bought them, I hate to encourage pothunters, but I couldn't resist. I like to look at them while I'm working."

"They're similar to some of the things missing from David's office."

"I'm not surprised," she said, grabbing her messenger bag from her worktable and throwing it over her shoulder. "They're hardly rare, especially the pots and the pipe. I doubt you'll ever recover Dr. Morgan's property. It'll be sold by now."

She was telling the truth. Simon was deeply, happily relieved.

"I'll call you this afternoon," he said. "After I'm through," and he felt the weight of his duties settle on his shoulders, "with Denise McGrath."

ON HIS WAY TO work Simon stopped by his house to pick up his briefcase. He found Rex standing in the middle of the living room. Just standing, facing the door, disappointed again.

"I'm sorry, buddy," Simon said, patting his head. The dog shoved his nose into Simon's hand, but didn't wag his tail. Simon picked up his briefcase and went to the door, then stopped and looked back. Rex still stood in the middle of the floor, looking past Simon, out the front door, waiting.

"Look," Simon said to him, as if he were a person, "why don't you come to work with me? You could use a change of scenery." Maybe the dog was bored. Morgan had taken his dogs everywhere with him.

Simon found Rex's leash and, remembering the dog's arthritis, an old blanket, and led him out to his Thunderbird. On the way to campus Rex sat quietly next to Simon on the passenger seat, his head even with Simon's, staring straight ahead out the windshield, for all the world like a human being who wasn't in the mood for conversation.

On the walk from the parking lot to the historic limestone building that housed Kenan's history department, Rex's ears pricked up a couple of times, once at a squirrel madly scooping up pecans and again at a yellow leaf that floated down right in front of his nose.

Once in Simon's office Rex curled up on his blanket on the floor next to Simon's chair, and Simon turned his attention to his work. A number of envelopes, obviously containing notes or sympathy cards, lay scattered over the desk. They were from his colleagues and some of his students, even one from his nemesis, Vera Thayer, full professor of European intellectual history and pedant. Very kind of them all, he thought, scooping the notes, unopened, into a top drawer.

What did he need to do today? His North Carolina history class met later this morning. The students should have completed fifty pages of reading, which he'd placed on reserve at the library, on the conflict between loyalist and revolutionary factions in the state prior to the Revolution. He hadn't prepared a quiz, so he needed to locate a lecture he could deliver today instead.

A neat stack of papers rested on a corner of his desk, thoughtfully collected by someone from the class he'd missed on Tuesday. He required a five-page bimonthly paper from his students in Introduction to American History, on a topic he assigned. This batch was an essay on anti-federalist opposition to the ratification of the Constitution. He'd always wondered if the Constitution would have been ratified if Jefferson, its main opponent, hadn't been in France at the time. It was a rare student who tumbled to that coincidence.

SIMON WOULD GRADE THE papers over the weekend. He wanted to spend the evening with Martha. It was good to have something to look forward to again.

Walker Jones nudged open Simon's door, a Thermos

bottle in one hand, two mugs in the other, and a carton of cream wedged under his elbow.

"Good morning," he said.

"Hi, Walker, come in."

"Fresh coffee for both of us," he said. "From my private stock—Costa Rican. I'll even let you ruin it with all that cream and sugar you use."

"Thanks. I haven't had nearly enough caffeine this morning."

He pushed aside papers and books so Walker could set the coffee paraphernalia down on his desk, and found packets of sugar in one of his desk drawers.

Walker pulled up a chair. "You doing okay?"

"Yeah," he said. "At least the funeral's over."

Walker noticed Rex. "Who's your new friend?" he asked.

"One of Morgan's dogs," Simon said, "Rex. I gave the younger one to my next-door neighbor. This one is so depressed, I think I'm going to have to consult the vet about it. I understand there are such things as canine anti-depressants."

"Animals grieve, there's no doubt about it."

At the sound of Walker's voice, Rex cocked his head and looked up at him. Walker reached down and scratched him on the top of his head. To Simon's surprise, Rex moved his tail a little. Walker leaned forward in his chair and used both hands to rub behind the old dog's ears.

"He's pretty old," Simon said. "I may need to keep him myself. I don't think he's adoptable."

"He's not as old as all that. I'll bet he's got a few good years left in him."

Rex stood up creakily and leaned against Walker's knees.

"I'll be damned," Simon said. "He hasn't done anything like that since I brought him home."

"Something about me must remind him of Dr. Morgan," Walker said. "Do you really want to keep him?"

Hope sprang in Simon's breast.

"I'd be delighted to find him a good home," Simon said. "I have my cats, you know. Are you saying you want him?"

"I just might," Walker said. He rooted around in his jacket pocket and found a red-striped peppermint, which he unwrapped. "My old border collie died last year. He used to love these things," he said, flipping the mint to Rex. Rex caught it and crunched it happily, then rested a front paw on Walker's arm.

"You two are made for each other," Simon said.

"I think so, too," Walker said. "I've been wanting another dog, and this one's just my speed."

"You'll need to give him a buffered aspirin twice a day for his arthritis," Simon said.

"I've got an economy-sized bottle at home. Can I take him now?"

"Absolutely." Simon handed over the leash and blanket, and watched the dog and his new master leave his office, Rex's tail wagging like a windshield washer.

Another burden relieved, Simon turned his attention to searching his file cabinet for his lecture on the Battle of Moore's Creek Bridge.

———

AFTER HIS CLASS SIMON found Jack Kingfisher waiting for him in the hall outside the lecture room. Kingfisher was an assistant professor of American history, specializing in Native American and minority studies. He also taught a Civil War course, giving students a perspective on the conflict they hadn't had before. Jack was an authority on the Thomas Legion, the Sixty-ninth Regiment of North Carolina, a Confederate battalion containing two companies of Cherokee Indians.

Kingfisher was himself a Cherokee Indian who grew up on the Qualla Boundary, the reservation in western North Carolina. He was lean and muscular, with glossy black hair cut short, prominent cheekbones, and olive skin. He wore a blue oxford cloth shirt with the sleeves rolled up, tucked into baggy khakis, and athletic shoes with no socks.

"Welcome back," Simon said to him. "How was the conference?"

"It was good," Kingfisher said, shaking Simon's hand. "But I was so sorry to hear about your friend. How tragic."

"Thanks."

"Sophie tells me you wanted to talk to me?"

"Morgan was on the committee to decide what to do with Uwharrie Man."

"Whoa," Kingfisher said. "You think that had something to do with his death? I heard he interrupted a burglary."

"A burglar who stole all his notes on Uwharrie Man? A burglar who drugged his dogs with allergy tablets? A burglar who stole a wallet, a few Indian artifacts, and left behind a CD player and a laptop? Morgan was the tie-breaker on that committee. No matter which way he decided, his decision would ruin careers."

"You want my take on Uwharrie Man?"

"Yes, if you've got time. Have you had lunch yet?"

THE TWO MEN FOUND a corner table for two in the faculty dining room and emptied their cafeteria trays. They'd both picked a Kenan College cafeteria specialty, homemade chili with cracklin' corn bread.

"So," Kingfisher said, liberally buttering his corn bread, "what do you want to know?"

"Start with why the Lumbee and Brad Lowery feel so strongly about this."

"Well, everyone knows that Brad wants to run for Congress, and making all this noise about Uwharrie Man keeps him in the public eye. Serving on the Tribal Council just doesn't give him the scope he needs."

"Cynic."

"Not really. He'd be a good congressman."

"About the graves law . . ."

"The state law is based on the federal statute that protects Native American burials and graveyards. It's meant to protect burials from collectors and pothunters."

"That's a problem?"

"You have no idea. 'Scavenging' is a gentle word for what goes on. It all started with the Victorians. They were shameless collectors; you know how they used Darwin's theories to justify abusing the 'inferior' races. After nineteenth century frontier battles, American soldiers would load up the corpses of Indians killed in battle on wagons and take them straight to museums in the East, where, to put it delicately, they were rendered down into skeletons, measured, catalogued, and displayed. Do you know where the term 'redskins' came from? I'll give you a hint—it doesn't refer to our ruddy complexions."

"Then I have no idea."

"In the old days, when there was a bounty on Indians, the term was coined to refer to their bloody corpses. Kind of like coonskins refer to raccoon hides."

"Not one of our country's finest hours."

"Then after the Indians were sent to the reservations, collectors excavated their graveyards and historic settlements. There are literally hundreds of Indian skeletons and thousands of the artifacts that were buried with them in museums and private collections all over the country. Even today there's virtually no protection of burials and graveyards. How would you like to have a great-grandparent dug up and sold on eBay? It happens. So Indians use the federal and state grave protection laws to stop anthropologists from excavating any human remains. They're fed up with being 'studied.' They want ownership of their own history and religion. They want human remains treated respectfully and want to have a say over what happens to artifacts and archaeological sites."

Simon fetched an iced-tea pitcher from a buffet and poured them both fresh glasses.

"Surely the law wasn't meant to protect human remains thousands of years old, like Uwharrie Man," Simon said. "Fourteen thousand years ago—that's deep time—there's no way to say what tribe, if any, is related to that skeleton."

"You can say that, but Indians believe that disturbing the dead upsets the cycle of life, that it has spiritual consequences. I'm a secular Indian, but I was raised on the reservation, and I've visited archaeological digs, and I'm very uncomfortable in the presence of human remains, no matter how old they are. My tribe, the eastern band of the Cherokee, has claimed hundreds of Cherokee remains since these laws were passed, and reburied all of them."

"I think I understand Brad Lowery's position a little better."

"Then there's the racial angle," Kingfisher said. "You know that some of the oldest remains found, the ones that predate the Siberian land bridge crossings, appear to have Caucasian features?"

"Like Kennewick Man."

"Yeah, well, racists use these remains as evidence that Indians weren't the first colonizers of America, so we shouldn't get the so-called benefits of being Native Americans."

"I have heard that before," Simon said, but he refrained from repeating Mabry's words.

"But scientists know that we, meaning the American Indians who occupied this country when the Europeans arrived here, are the genetic descendants of the Siberians. If there were people here earlier from other parts of the world, and I think there were, we won and they lost. They didn't survive, genetically speaking."

"How does Uwharrie Man fit into this scenario?" Simon asked.

Jack gestured with his spoon as he talked. "If Uwharrie Man descended from European Caucasians, and if the pre-Clovis spear point found with him is culturally derived from the Solutrean in France, does that mean that white people invented the Clovis culture in America? That would mean, you see, that the Indians overwhelmed the whites, but adopted their culture. Get it? White people are smarter than Indians."

"That's an extreme position."

"Yes, but that doesn't stop people from saying it."

"I've lost track of your point."

"It's possible that Brad Lowery thinks that a skeletal analysis of Uwharrie Man might show that Caucasians were in North Carolina before Indians. The right-wing crazies would have a field day with that kind of information."

SIMON PICKED UP MORGAN's life insurance check from the state personnel office and deposited it in the estate account. He reimbursed himself for the money he'd spent on the estate's expenses, adding up his receipts three times to make sure he had the correct amount. Then he wrote a check out of the estate account for thirty-five thousand dollars and took it to Morgan's house to give to Denise McGrath.

He found her loading Morgan's truck parked in the driveway. She wasn't taking much, just a few cardboard file boxes. Simon heaved the last of them onto the truck bed for her.

"Mostly pictures," Denise said. "And I've got copies of David's books and articles, and some of his tools. I want my boys to have them. I want them to remember my brother."

Simon handed her the check. To give her some credit, she didn't look at the amount before she folded it into her wallet. But then she knew about what it would be.

"I'm leaving you with a lot of work to do," she said.

"I'm sorry. I just have to get home. I'm going to drive straight through."

"It's okay," Simon said. "Goes with the job."

She gave him back her set of the house keys.

"If I find anything else in the house I think you or your sons might like, I'll call you," Simon said.

They shook hands, and Simon watched as she backed the big truck out of the driveway and drove down the street, turning at Oberlin Road to catch I-40 all the way to Knoxville, Tennessee.

Simon really hoped she hadn't killed her brother.

He unlocked the house and went inside, where for two hours he systematically searched the house from top to bottom, even pulling down the ladder to the attic, which was empty except for spiderwebs and a thick layer of dust, looking for Morgan's notes on Uwharrie Man, again. Still he found nothing.

Simon washed the attic dirt off his hands in the kitchen sink. Why was he so sure those notes had been stolen by Morgan's murderer? He had, as Otis Gates had emphasized, no firm evidence to support that. In fact, there was no firm evidence to support any theory of this crime. All of which reminded him of Seneca's musings on motive: "He who profits by villainy, has perpetrated it."

Someone who benefited from Morgan's death murdered him, and Simon wouldn't rest until the killer was found.

9

What? The flames already?

—VOLTAIRE'S LAST WORDS (1778),

AS THE BEDSIDE LAMP FLARED UP

SIMON LET HIMSELF INTO HIS HOUSE. HIS CATS WERE BACK in residence, all three of them curled up in their usual and customary locations: a corner of the sofa, the puddle of sunlight on top of the baby grand, and the chair closest to the fireplace. They ignored him, still vexed with him for introducing, however briefly, two canines into their home. They barely condescended to eat the kibble he dished into their bowls.

Simon poured himself a weak bourbon and Coke and went out onto his porch, carrying his phone with him in case Martha called. He'd thought about her all day, with pleasure and anticipation. Of course, they had just met, but they'd felt like a couple to him from the minute he'd picked her up at her apartment last night. It helped that the two of them fit together like a deadbolt lock during lovemaking. No one could predict love was in their future after just one evening, but the potential was there and he was optimistic. He felt like his love affair with Julia might had been over for months instead of days.

His phone rang. It was Martha. He welcomed the rush of warmth and intimacy he felt when he heard her voice.

"Hi, sweetie," she said.

"Hi yourself," he said. "Where are you? What do you want to do tonight? I'll come pick you up."

"I can't believe I forgot about this, but I need to stay in Chapel Hill this evening. Dr. Mabry's delivering an endowed lecture tonight, and I have to be there."

"Let me guess—you're running the PowerPoint presentation? In my day it was the slide projector."

"We haven't even finished the damn thing yet. I'll be clicking away madly, gnawing on an energy bar, while he presides over the cocktail buffet. I'm so sorry. It slipped my mind completely."

"Don't worry about it. Tomorrow?"

"For sure."

"Why don't you pick up some things at your apartment on the way and plan to spend the rest of the weekend here?"

"I'll be at your house by noon."

SIMON WAS DISAPPOINTED HE wouldn't see Martha tonight, but he understood her predicament. There was no end to the drudgery expected of graduate students. And all her hard work would be in vain if Martha couldn't finish her dissertation. For her sake he hoped the committee could find a way to turn the remains of Uwharrie Man over to Mabry and the museum. He didn't intend to say so publicly, but he supported analyzing the remains, and he believed that Morgan would agree with him. He didn't see how Uwharrie Man, hundreds of generations removed from people alive today, could be considered an ancestor of any modern tribe. There was no evidence at all that the artifacts found with him were grave goods, or that his burial was a religious event. Prehistoric remains shouldn't belong to any particular interest group, but to the human species, all of whom have a stake in understanding the evolution of human cultures. There was precedent for his position. Recently a federal court turned down the claims of five Northwest Indian tribes for the skeleton of Kennewick Man, and released the remains to anthropologists for study.

Simon didn't much like Lawrence Mabry, but he was a scientist. He had less sympathy for Lowery's motives. With a pang of guilt he acknowledged to himself that he hadn't spent enough time with Lowery to judge him.

Simon was hungry. He loaded a plate from the containers of funeral food left in his refrigerator and stuck it in the microwave. He passed on another bourbon. If he couldn't see Martha tonight, he wanted to go over Morgan's computer files and papers again. Perhaps he'd missed something.

After he'd eaten and settled on his sofa, Simon flicked on the gas fire and opened Morgan's old canvas briefcase. He owned it now, which gave him a creepy sensation.

Morgan's work, his books, papers, and files, would soon be part of the permanent collection of the Kenan College Library. Short of an apocalypse the collection would remain there for generations. No wonder people left legacies. Consciousness of human mortality drove them to leave something behind so they wouldn't be forgotten, children, art, great public buildings, whatever. It certainly created a disposal problem for their executors.

Don't think so much, Simon admonished himself. There was nothing to gain from being mawkish. More productive to get to work and accomplish something.

He flipped through the journals in Morgan's briefcase. Here were the articles Julia had mentioned, one on the use of ore petrography to trace the source of stone tools to a specific quarry, another on using DNA from animal hides to calculate a prehistoric clan's hunting range. Both technologies were extremely expensive and rarely used. The single file folder in the briefcase contained a copy of the North Carolina statute "Indian Antiquities, Archaeological Resources and Unmarked Human Skeletal Remains Protection." Reviewing Morgan's planner and cell phone memory yielded nothing new.

Simon revisited the Internet bookmarks Morgan had saved during the wee hours of the morning of his death. There were dozens of them, with titles like "Paleoamerican Origins," "Models of Migration to the New World," "Pre-Columbian Trans-oceanic Contact," "Ore Petrography and Archaeological Provenance," "Fundamentals of Radio Carbon Dating," and "The Antiquity of Humankind in the Americas." After staying up all night doing this research, Morgan had been interrupted in his office by his killer. Gates would say there was no evidence that the two events, Morgan's research and his murder, were related. But still Simon's instincts told him there was a connection, mostly because of Morgan's missing notes.

For God's sake, where were those damned notes? They might tell him why Morgan had been studying this material all night, what he thought of it, of the committee and its charge, and how he intended to vote on the control of Uwharrie Man's mortal remains. If the notes had been stolen by the murderer, then the murder and the committee's work must be connected. If they weren't stolen, where the hell were they? He slammed both hands on the coffee table in frustration, sending his cats flying out of their comfortable niches. He was exhausted with wondering about those notes. They were never out of his thoughts.

Simon didn't sleep well that night, and woke up the next morning too early. He drank three cups of coffee and took his shower, dressed, and decided to tidy up his house in preparation for Martha's arrival at noon. He took his laptop and Morgan's briefcase up to his study on the second floor.

Simon reached for the power cord to his laptop to charge it, but it wasn't where he usually left it, draped over a mug containing pens and pencils, to keep it from dropping to the floor where the wheels of his office chair tended to roll over it. In fact, the mug was out of place, too, on the wrong side of the desk. He took a deep breath, then scanned the entire room. Someone had searched his study, carefully, but still the signs were unmistakable. The key to his file cabinet was in the wrong compartment in his desk drawer, so he concluded his files had been rifled. The stack of blue books he needed to grade, which rested on top of yet another stack of papers, had been shuffled. He knew that because he'd noticed that Maya Ott's paper had topped the stack and he hoped she hadn't cheated this time, since he didn't have the energy to deal with an honor court. Now Ellen Harris's paper capped the stack of blue books.

While Simon slept the deep sleep of a satiated lover the other night, Martha had left his bed to snoop around his office, looking for Morgan's notes, he supposed. Had she thought of it herself? Had she planned to seduce him to get access to his study? Had Mabry suggested it?

Simon was deeply disappointed. The fragile bubble of their possible future together burst. Simon lifted up his telephone receiver to call Otis Gates.

"I WISH YOU'D LEAVE police work to the police," Gates said. Gates's cubicle just barely contained the big man, his desk, a file cabinet, and the one chair Simon occupied. Gates leaned back in his own chair, long legs stretching under his desk, fiddling with a pencil. He'd loosened his tie, which betrayed his stress levels, since little disturbed Gates's sartorial perfection.

"Don't you see?" Simon said. "Martha Dunn carries water for Lawrence Mabry, so if she is searching my house for Morgan's notes, that means Mabry doesn't have them, which means that he didn't kill Morgan, and neither did she, and neither did Henry Klett, probably."

"You don't know she was looking for the notes."

"What else could it be?"

"You deduce from this superabundance of conclusive evidence that Brad Lowery killed Dr. Morgan to keep him from voting to hand over the skeleton to the museum."

"Lowery was in town for the committee meeting. His hotel is only a few blocks from Morgan's house. He could have been out early, have seen Morgan's light on, stopped to talk to him, and when he realized how he was going to vote, killed him and stole his notes."

"You're obsessed with those notes. Forget the damn notes. Where is the real evidence? Every single one of the members of the committee were in town that morning—none of them has an alibi. If you were yourself, you'd realize how full of holes your theory is."

"Listen, everyone involved thought Morgan would vote with Mabry and Klett. The three of them would vote down Lambert and Lowery. This is Lowery's last chance at a congressional nomination. If he loses it, he'll likely never get another opportunity. He needs to prove to his Lumbee constituents that he has influence. I'm guessing he wants the governor to appoint a new committee to keep the controversy alive."

" 'Guess' is not a word we use much in homicide investigation," Gates said. He leaned over his desk, pointing his forefinger at Simon. "I'm acting on real evidence, Simon, not speculation, like, Denise McGrath doesn't have an alibi."

"What? She told me she was going to fax some receipts for her hotel to you."

"Now she says she can't find them. She claims the cleaning woman threw them out while she was gone. There's not a scrap of paper, not a phone call, not a witness, that proves she attended that teachers' conference. She's the one with the compelling interest in Dr. Morgan's death. The Knoxville police are interviewing her now, and executing a search warrant on her home and vehicles. A Knoxville homicide detective working at her house called me right before you came in and told me there are hundreds of unexplained miles on her automobile."

"Oh, hell."

"You mark my words," Gates said. "Denise McGrath killed her brother. She faked attending that conference, drove up here, and bludgeoned him to death with the geode. Then she took his wallet and a couple of trinkets and drugged the dogs to make it look like a botched robbery. That's where the evidence is."

Simon had no words.

"You stay out of this," Otis continued. "Any police officer would excuse himself from investigating a friend's death, and you should, too." He tapped his pencil on the file open on his desk. "Let me have Martha Dunn's address," he said.

"What for?"

"You've told me that she searched your study, that she possesses artifacts that looked like the ones stolen from Dr. Morgan's house. I need to question her," Gates said. "It's procedure. I don't think it will be relevant to the murder, but I don't let my feelings interfere with my job."

Simon gave Gates Martha's address and phone number. She wouldn't speak to him again even if he wanted her to. He'd just add Martha to the growing list of women who'd never warm his bed again.

Gates didn't walk Simon to the door of the police station, or offer him a cup of coffee, or tell him he'd let him know the results of his interview with Martha. How many friends and lovers had he lost this week? Morgan, Julia, Martha, maybe Otis, too. Four more than he could afford.

As he walked to the parking lot and his car, his cell phone rang. It was Dale Cousins, librarian at his local public library, telling him that she'd found a yellow pad covered with notes in Dr. David Morgan's handwriting, and she understood Simon was his executor, and did he want to come pick it up?

As embarrassed as he'd ever been in his life, Simon went back inside to tell Gates that Morgan had left his notes in the library before he died. Brad Lowery hadn't stolen them, and neither had anyone else.

DAVID MORGAN HAD A cheap streak. He stopped by the library every week to read the magazines he was too frugal to subscribe to. On his last visit his yellow pad must have slipped out of his briefcase and slid under a bank of chairs, where Cousins found it.

"I noticed his name on the front cover. And of course I knew he had died recently. Such an awful thing. I thought the notes might be important to someone," she said.

"Thank you," Simon said, as he took the pad from her.

Simon sat down at a table in a corner and read Morgan's notes on Uwharrie Man. As he expected, Morgan advocated allowing the museum to keep, and Dr. Lawrence Mabry to study, the remains of Uwharrie Man. Interspersed among his more objective notes, Morgan wrote what he thought of the issue: *Uwharrie Man was found on state property, which belongs to all North Carolinians,* and then *the government has the responsibility to see that important fossils are put in institutional hands, not private cupboards,* and again, *I don't see that anyone can connect Uwharrie Man to the modern Lumbee Nation,* and again, *there is no evidence that this is a burial in any religious sense of the word.*

The only responsible thing for Simon to do was to call the committee members and tell them what he had found. Outside the library, he leaned up against his car and pulled out his cell phone.

Henry Klett was elated. "Dr. Mabry is right here with me," he said. "We are both so pleased. Thank you for calling us."

"What's next for the committee?" Simon asked.

"Of course Dr. Morgan's expressed opinion doesn't count as a vote, but it should help work out a compromise. I'm going over several ideas with Dr. Mabry. I think what you've found will help us convince Brad Lowery."

SIMON CLICKED OFF HIS cell phone, then dialed information for Lumberton, North Carolina, to get Lowery's telephone number and tell him that Morgan's notes had been found. It was only fair that he let him know as soon as he told Klett and Mabry. The operator at the hospital where Lowery worked as a pharmacist told Simon that she couldn't page Lowery during his shift for any reason other than an emergency.

The adrenaline that had fueled Simon since the morning, when he'd discovered that Martha had searched his office, was leaking away, leaving him worn out and depressed. He checked his watch. Eleven o'clock. Martha was due at his place in an hour, except that when she got to her apartment to pack for the weekend, she'd find the police waiting there to question her.

Simon got into his car, but didn't turn on the ignition. He leaned his head back on the seat, closing his eyes, trying to block out the ugly thoughts that preoccupied him.

How much of their date was an act? Had Martha slept with him just to get access to his house? Had it really been necessary for him to turn her in to the police? Or had he done it out of hurt and anger? Neither of them could take what they'd done back.

And Simon was bothered by the fact that he couldn't get through to Lowery to tell him about finding Morgan's notes. He barely knew the man, but still suspected him of murder, and had said as much to the police. The least he could do was give Lowery a heads-up about the notes, keep Mabry and Klett from having the advantage of surprise.

He checked his watch again. It was only about two hours to Lumberton. He could be there to talk to Lowery when he got off his shift, and warn him that Klett and Mabry would use Morgan's notes against him. Though Simon tended to agree with them, he did believe that ethics were important in history and archaeology, and that Lowery should have a chance to prepare a final defense of his position.

Besides, if Simon left town, he could get away from today's emotional disasters for a little while. He might even spend the night away, or go on to the beach for the weekend. Maybe he would get some sleep if he was out of town.

Simon's cell phone rang. It was Martha. He didn't answer. He'd talk to her eventually, he just didn't have the courage right this minute. Instead he got in his Thunderbird and headed south, one of Morgan's Nickel Creek CDs blasting. He didn't stop for lunch. He'd lost his appetite again.

The Lumbee Indians had been much in the news lately, campaigning for federal recognition. The Lumbee didn't live on a reservation, never fought a battle with the United States, and never signed a treaty with the United States government. The tribe had over forty thousand enrolled members, most living in Robeson County and its adjacent counties, the largest American Indian tribe east of the Mississippi River. Their history, or rather their history according to white historians, was less than three hundred years old. The Lumbee were first "discovered" by European explorers living in the swamps of southeastern North Carolina in 1725, along the banks of Drowning

Creek, now known as the Lumber River. The Lumbee wore white man's clothing, lived in log cabins, spoke "Lumbee English," practiced Christianity, and bore English surnames. They were clearly of mixed race, many with blue eyes, so clearly mixed-race that they weren't forced to walk the "Trail of Tears" to Oklahoma with other Native Americans in the 1820s and 1830s.

For years anthropologists classed the Lumbee as just one of many triracial isolates that evolved from the intermarriage of whites, blacks, and Indians in a restricted geographic location, like the Melungeons and the Redbone, but their story may be far more interesting than that. The Lumbee almost certainly descended from the Croatan Indians of Hatteras Island, who absorbed the Lost Colony when it abandoned Roanoke Island between 1587 and 1590. When Sir Walter Raleigh returned to Roanoke Island in 1590 with desperately needed supplies for his colony, he found only ruins and the letters *Croatan* carved into a tree. It's a standing joke among the Lumbee, that they don't understand why the Roanoke Colony is called the Lost Colony, since they left a note saying where they were going. It's not a coincidence that English surnames common among the Lumbee, names like Locklear, Chavis, Oxendine, Bullard, and Lowery, are the same as many of the surnames of the Roanoke colonists. During the nineteenth century the Lumbee tribe offered sanctuary to runaway slaves, bringing African-American genes into the mix.

In the nineteenth century North Carolina was an unpleasant place to live if your skin was dark, but the Lumbee resisted subjugation, sometimes violently. In the 1860s Lumbee folk hero Henry Berry Lowrie, incensed by the assault and murder of family members by whites, spent a decade wreaking vigilante justice on those who harassed Indians. He was never caught. And a century later, on one night in January 1958, a contingent of armed Lumbee confronted the Ku Klux Klan, who were rallying to intimidate Indians, and demanded they leave Robeson County. When the Klansmen refused, the Lumbee routed them, chasing them into the woods and out of the county. The fleeing Klan members left behind their flag, a few discarded white robes, and a cross they hadn't had time to ignite. The Klan never returned to Robeson County.

During the Jim Crow era, Robeson County had three school systems, white, black, and Indian. The Lumbee founded Croatan Normal School, which became Pembroke State College, the first state-supported four-year college for Indians in the country. It's now the University of North Carolina at Pembroke, which grants the only major in American Indian studies in the country.

Once Simon drove into Robeson County, he became an outsider. The county was almost half Indian. The town of Pembroke, where Lowery lived, was over eighty percent Indian. Lumberton, the county seat, where Lowery worked at the medical center, was a few miles to the east.

AT THE MEDICAL CENTER Simon waited for Lowery in the pharmacy office. The young woman at the desk told him Lowery couldn't leave without passing through, and his shift wasn't quite over yet. Sure enough, Lowery came through a few minutes after the hour, stripping off his blue pharmacist's coat.

"What are you doing here?" he asked Simon.

"I need to talk to you," Simon said.

"You heard of telephones?"

"Let's just say the drive was therapeutic."

"Come on in here. There's coffee."

Lowery led Simon into a tiny lounge, where he filled up two mugs with coffee. The coffee must have been stewing on its burner for hours. The sugar and cream Simon added to his made it barely drinkable.

"Okay," Lowery said, sitting down in a battered chair, a refugee from some eighties medical waiting room, indicating another one to Simon, "sit down and get to the point. I want to go home."

"I found my friend's notes," Simon said.

"Oh, hell," he said. "Let me guess, they make his position clear?"

"Very."

"You came down here to tell me I'm now officially fighting a lost cause? Thanks."

"The hospital switchboard wouldn't put me through to you, and I didn't want Mabry and Klett to have the advantage of knowing the contents of the notes earlier than you did."

"That's white of you."

"Don't mention it."

"What did Klett say?"

"That he was working on a compromise. Are you going to hear him out?"

"What choice do I have?" Lowery said. "I never had much chance of blocking them. If those notes hadn't shown up, the governor would have appointed another archaeologist to the committee, and he'd support the rest of the scientists."

"You use the word 'scientist' like it was a dirty word."

"I'm a pharmacist, I'm a scientist myself, but there's a place for it. White anthropologists and archaeologists have been co-opting our history and culture for centuries, explaining to the world what the Indian is about, building their careers on our backs. Every summer we have to dodge all the anthropology students prowling around down here looking for thesis topics. They're worse than the tourists. We're sick of it. We're not extinct, we're not going the way of the mammoth. We want control of our own history."

"Uwharrie Man is over fourteen thousand years old. He's hardly Lumbee."

"He was found in the eastern part of the state where our Cherow ancestors lived. The Lumbee inherit him by default."

"Some people might say your motives are political."

"Of course they're political, don't be naive. And yeah, I do want to go to Congress, what's wrong with that? I want to represent the Lumbee in a national setting. We want to build a casino like the Cherokee have, and create jobs so our young people can work here and we can continue to live as a tribe."

"How does burying Uwharrie Man help you do that?"

"Even other Indian tribes claim we're not really Native American, that our history is only three hundred years old, but you and I both know we're what's left of the Croatan and Cherow nations. If we claim Uwharrie Man successfully, that establishes our credibility as a tribe."

"And if you rebury the remains, no one can discover that he's a European. For God's sake, we're all mongrels, you're lighter than I am. The Indians who occupied North America when the Europeans arrived in the fifteenth century descended from the Asian people who entered across the Bering Strait. Genetics prove that. No one can take that away from you."

"That won't stop some from trying."

THE YOUNG WOMAN FROM the front desk rapped on the door before opening it.

"You're popular today, Brad," she said. "You've got more company." Henry Klett stood behind her.

"Where's Lawrence Mabry?" Lowery asked. "Then you'll really outnumber me."

Klett stretched out a hand to Lowery, and when he didn't take it, grabbed his arm.

"It's not like that," Klett said. "I have a compromise I want to propose. The museum has no interest in offending the Native American community."

Simon got up, intending to leave.

"No," Klett said, "don't go yet. I'd like your perspective. You know best what Dr. Morgan might have agreed to."

Lowery nodded at Simon, indicating he could stay.

Klett sat down, placing his hands flat on the table.

"I've learned a lot from this experience," Klett said, "and I've come to believe that scientists must deal with human bones in a more respectful and sensitive manner."

"That's something."

"I propose that we follow the example of the Sandy Hill excavation."

"The Pequot tribe, in Connecticut. What do you suggest?"

"That the Lumbee Nation appoint a Native American anthropologist as codirector of the study with Dr. Mabry, and after the study is complete, the museum will return Uwharrie Man and his artifacts to the Lumbee nation."

Lowery chewed on his lower lip.

"We can nominate whomever we want? From the University at Pembroke?"

"Yes, absolutely."

"Mabry agrees with this?"

"I don't know if I can say so right now. I told him I intend to push this compromise with the governor."

"It may be doable," Lowery said. "It's better than having yet another Indian skeleton displayed in a museum. You'll have to get Brenda Lambert on board. Have you talked to her about this?

"She's not in Raleigh, she's in Cherokee for a meeting. But I'm willing to go out there today if you give me the green light."

"Okay. What the hell. Go ahead. Let's hear what she says."

"Why don't you come with me?"

"I can't. I'm working another shift tonight. Got to go home and get some sleep."

Klett turned to Simon.

"Are you free? Why don't you come with me? I know Brad would like to have a disinterested observer when Ms. Lambert and I talk."

"Are you going today?" Simon said. "It's a long drive. And I have my own car here."

"Not a problem," Klett said. "I brought my airplane."

10

... codeine ... bourbon ...

—THE LAST WORDS OF TALLULAH BANKHEAD (1902–1968),
ACTRESS BEST KNOWN FOR HER ROLE IN *LIFEBOAT*

SIMON AND LOWERY ADMIRED KLETT'S AIRPLANE. THE sleek machine was painted white topside and shadow-gray on its underbelly, the body colors divided by two swooshing stripes, one red and one blue. It had a single three-blade propeller. Sitting in the sunlight on the apron, the airplane just plain gleamed, radiating an aura of adventure and power.

Lowery had postponed his nap to drive them to the Lumberton Municipal Airport, and now he walked slowly around the plane, running his hands over the fuselage.

"How fast?" Simon asked Klett.

"I cruise at a hundred fifty miles an hour or so."

Lowery ducked under the propeller and circled the aircraft again. "How long have you been flying?" he asked.

"Since I was fifteen. I've owned this plane for, oh, about ten years now." He stroked a wingtip affectionately. "It's my baby. My wife and I fly somewhere almost every weekend. We go to the beach or to visit our daughter in college. Sometimes we take it up to Washington when there's something at the Kennedy Center we want to see."

"I wish I could go with you," Lowery said. "Flying west this time of year, the scenery will be magnificent."

"I'll be glad to take you up another time," Klett said. "It's always beautiful."

Klett opened the door of the plane and pulled out two heavy fuel cans from behind the back seats. He unscrewed the caps and checked to make sure both were full, then stowed them in the plane again.

"There isn't any gas available at the Bryson City airfield," he said, moving around to the other side of the plane, opening both gas tanks, and peering inside. "I told the maintenance guys here to make sure the cans and both tanks are full. It never hurts to do a visible check."

"Bryson City?" Simon asked.

"It's a private airport, just a few miles from Cherokee," Klett said. "Brenda Lambert said she'd pick us up. I told her I'd call her when we're ten minutes out."

Simon and Lowery admired the airplane while Klett completed his preflight check. Excitement overshadowed any nervousness Simon felt about flying in the small craft. Besides, this trip with Klett was a good excuse to postpone going home, where the heartbreak of Morgan's murder and the mess he'd made by involving himself in the case simmered, waiting for him.

His cell phone rang. Martha's number appeared on the screen. He didn't answer it. Whether she was angry, conciliatory, or apologetic, he just couldn't deal with her. He'd talk with her eventually, but he needed a break to rebuild his emotional reserves.

"Hey, Simon," Klett said, and pointed to the door to the men's restroom across the hangar. "Always go before taking off," he said. "No facilities aboard."

Lowery was still standing by the airplane when they returned to it. He stuck out his hand to shake both theirs.

"Good luck," he said. "I'll think of you while I'm passing out pills tonight."

"I'll call you tomorrow and let you know what Ms. Lambert says," Klett said.

Lowery waved at them as he walked off the tarmac toward his car.

"Climb on in," Klett said to Simon. Simon pulled himself into the passenger side of the cockpit. Klett strapped himself in with a lap belt and a shoulder harness, and Simon followed suit. Klett slipped on his dark glasses.

"There's a spare pair of sunglasses in there," he said, indicating a compartment on Simon's door. "It can get right bright above the clouds. You've got a set of flight controls on your side of the plane, too. After we take off you can fly her, if you like."

"Absolutely," Simon said. "You don't have to offer twice."

They taxied down the runway and turned around to face the long straight stretch of asphalt. As Klett increased power the airplane roared down the runway, then lifted into the air. Simon felt a surge of elation that drove every other sensation out of his body. He heard the wheels retract and their doors clang shut. Then the only sound was the roar of the engine, the whoosh of the propeller, and the rush of wind. The airport receded below them as they rose, and they soared over treetops alight with autumn foliage. The Carolina blue sky was clear and empty except for an occasional wisp of cloud floating by. Klett banked the airplane and headed west.

"Not bad, huh?" Klett said.

"It's such a different feeling from riding in a commercial airliner," Simon said. "More personal somehow."

"In one of those big jets you're insulated from the experience. Here you're in a tiny space, with just a thin metal skin between you and the sky, the power of the propeller and engine only a few feet in front of your seat."

After they reached altitude Klett turned the controls over to Simon. Switches and dials packed the dashboard in front of him. He'd never even been in a private plane before, much less flown one.

"This thing might as well be the space shuttle, as little as I know about all these gizmos," he said.

"Just use the wheel to keep the nose on the horizon and you'll be fine," Klett said. "I'll watch all the indicators."

After some wobbling Simon got the hang of it. Flying the plane was exhilarating, to say the least.

"Like it?" Klett asked.

"Hell, yes. What's not to like? How old is this airplane?"

"It's a 1978 Piper Archer, but the airframe just has eighteen hundred hours on it. I keep it in top condition. Just overhauled the engine, put in new cylinders, new mounts and bolts, and overhauled the alternator. Last year I installed an advanced GPS with a moving map display, but I never turn the damn thing on. I know my way around North Carolina by visual landmarks. There's a paper map in the compartment over there if you want to follow along."

Klett took the controls while Simon studied the map. He guessed they were already out of Robeson County and into Scotland County. If they traveled as the crow flies, they'd cross into South Carolina briefly before reentering North Carolina at Anson County, nip into South Carolina again south of Charlotte, then into North Carolina again around Brevard. They'd be well out of the swamps, sand-hills, and piedmont by then and flying into the Nantahala National Forest. The Cherokee Indian Reservation and Fontana Lake bordered Nantahala on the north, separating it from Great Smoky Mountains National Park.

North Carolina was a long state, stretching four hundred and seventy-five miles from the Outer Banks to the Tennessee line. Simon's mountain hometown of Boone was over a hundred miles to the northeast of their destination, in the Blue Ridge Mountains, just off the Blue Ridge Park-way. His father's family had lived there for so long no one remembered where they'd come from originally. His Aunt Rae Coffey and her daughter's family still farmed the orig-inal homeplace, making a good living growing Christmas trees and seasonal evergreens. Her son, Simon's cousin and childhood buddy Luther Coffey, owned an auto detail-ing business. Throughout the summer tourist season, when flatlanders visited to escape the heat, and into the fall, when the "leaf people" arrived to gawk at the foliage, Luther washed and polished BMWs and Mercedes and Jaguars, then spent the rest of the year hunting, fishing, and going to Appalachian State University football and basketball games.

Simon was overdue for a visit with them. Maybe he should rent a car in Cherokee and go up for a few days. That way he could postpone going back to Raleigh even longer. About three days was all he could stand to stay with Aunt Rae, although he could hang with Luther at his cabin for as much as a week before getting bored with country living. Walker Jones had said he could have a few more days off if he needed them. He'd plan to arrive after lunch on Sunday, so Aunt Rae couldn't pressure him into attending her little primitive Baptist Church. The potluck lunch after services was always delicious, a smorgasbord of country cooking, especially during homecoming, but she kept hoping he'd stand up one Sunday in the middle of the sermon, see the light, and beg to be baptized. He found it annoying that she expected him to go to hell, and besides, she cried over him.

The plane's radio started crackling.

"Charlotte airspace," Klett said. "Its not as bad as Atlanta yet, but the time is coming."

Klett slipped earphones over his head and took control of the airplane. Below them the flat fields and small towns became the golf courses and suburbs of the piedmont, and soon the ground began to rise. The subdivisions of Charlotte and Gastonia fell behind them, then rolling hills and pockets of dense forest appeared below.

"There's Brevard," Klett said, nodding below him at the college town nestled in the foothills of the Blue Ridge.

The plane continued to climb, following the topography of the land. Federal and state parks, interspersed with pockets of private property, a few small towns, and the Qualla Boundary, the Cherokee reservation, spread west from Brevard all the way to Tennessee and beyond. Simon felt chilly, and reached behind him into the back seat for his jacket. It was just a wool sport coat, but he was glad he had it.

"Did you hear the news about Dr. Morgan's sister before you left Raleigh?" Klett asked.

"Her alibi, a teachers' conference, hasn't been verified. She told me she had the paperwork at home and would fax it to Sergeant Gates when she got back to Tennessee."

"I hate to tell you this, Simon, but I don't want you to read it in the newspaper or hear it from a reporter. Denise McGrath's been arrested in Knoxville and held for extradition to Raleigh. She's been charged with murdering her brother. She wasn't at that conference."

Thank God Morgan would never know that his own sister had killed him for his life insurance. Simon could hardly bear it himself. And Denise's trial would be a dirty, nasty ordeal, fit only for a tacky television legal talk show. If she was convicted she'd spend the rest of her life in Women's Prison, just a few miles from Simon's house. He'd have to live knowing that.

"I'm sorry," Klett said. "I thought you should know."

"Thanks," Simon said. "I'm glad you told me."

Klett didn't say anything else, leaving Simon to face reality. Thinking Mabry or Lowery might have been involved in Morgan's murder was his imagination working overtime, his hope against hope, his defense against accepting that Morgan's sister was the obvious suspect in his murder. He supposed he could be forgiven for that, but Otis was right, he should never have involved himself in the investigation. What a mess he'd made of it all.

Adding insult to injury, he'd fallen for Martha Dunn on the rebound from losing Julia for good. The excellent evening they'd had was a lie. Martha had played him, bedded him, then searched his house in the middle of the night looking for Morgan's notes, which Mabry seemed to think he was holding back from the committee. He couldn't help wondering again if it was Martha's idea to seduce him, or if Mabry pimped her. Simon felt humiliated and disappointed.

On the other hand, he was flying west, leaving Raleigh far behind him, deep into the mountains. Grinning at him, Klett angled the airplane, dropped, flew between two tall transmission towers, then what seemed like straight up into the sky.

"Whoa," Simon said, gripping the arms of his seat.

"Thought you needed some distraction," Klett said.

"I did. Where are we?"

Suddenly the plane shuddered and dropped, maybe twenty feet, then stabilized.

"Jesus," Klett said.

Simon's stomach settled back into his abdomen after climbing into his throat.

"What was that?" Simon asked.

"No idea," Klett said. "But it's not good."

The plane shuddered again. Klett said nothing, struggling with the controls while the plane's nose dipped. The propeller stuttered.

Simon's body reacted to the sensation of falling out of the sky. Sweat broke out all over him and his gut twisted.

Klett reached above him and flipped a switch. The plane's engine engaged again and the propeller resumed its rhythmic rotation. Klett visibly relaxed.

"What happened?" Simon asked.

"I switched fuel tanks," Klett said. "There's plenty of fuel in the first tank, but it wasn't getting to the engine for some reason. We'll be fine, but I want us to land at Sylva."

"Okay," Simon said, forcing his voice to stay calm.

"There could be water in the tank," Klett said. "It collects there naturally. Although I had both tanks pumped out recently."

Simon thought Klett was trying to reassure himself as much as Simon.

The engine began to sputter again.

"Get in the back seat now," Klett said to him.

If Simon had been a bigger man he never could have squeezed between the front seats and the roof of the plane to get into the back. As it was, he was a tight fit.

"Get the fuel cans out of the back and jettison them," Klett said. "I want that fuel out of the plane."

"But I'll have to open the door."

"Yes, you will. Do it, quickly."

Simon reached behind the back seats into the narrow storage area inside the tail, grabbed a can, and forced open the door of the plane. A bitter wind lashed through the compartment. It took all Simon's strength to manhandle the fuel can out of the plane. Then he dragged the second can out from behind the rear seats and forced it outside, too. Pulling on the door handle with both hands, feet braced against the front seat, he was able to close and latch the door. He knew why Klett wanted the extra gasoline out of the plane: so it wouldn't add fuel to any fire that might break out if they crashed.

The engine still sputtered and they were noticeably closer to the ground.

Klett was on the radio, and Simon could hear it crackle in reply.

"I've let Atlanta Center know our position," Klett said. "There's no radio at Sylva, just an approach beacon."

"Are we going to crash?" Simon asked.

"Not if I can help it," Klett said.

Simon could see the sweat pouring down Klett's neck, his shoulder muscles bulging, his jaws clenched, as if he were engaged in some terrible physical effort. The engine engaged again and the plane began to climb.

"I don't know what's going on," Klett said. "The tanks are full, but fuel's not getting to the engine. Stay back there. Start to look for a clear area. We may have to make an emergency landing."

Simon saw nothing but ridges and ravines thick with trees and rock outcrops below him, and then he heard the engine sputter one last time and stop.

"We're gliding," Klett said. "I'm jettisoning the rest of the fuel in the tanks."

Simon wouldn't have selected the word "glide" to describe their descent. "Plummet" seemed a more appropriate choice.

"Stay in back," Klett said. "Check your seat belt, put your head between your knees, hunker down."

Simon did as he was told.

"This makes no sense," Klett said. "If I die and you don't, make sure the FAA examines these fuel tanks, hear me?"

"Yes," Simon said, "I will."

The airplane brushed the top of a tall pine, careened off it, then scraped the massive trunk of another, rolling to the side as it continued to fall.

"I'm so sorry," Klett said.

The plane's next impact with a tall pine tree sheared off one wing, and the airplane plunged, nose first, straight toward the forest floor. Simon bounced around the compartment, kept from breaking his neck by his seat belt, using his hands to fend off walls and roof, feeling intense pain in his ribs where the shoulder belt restrained him, his ankle turning sharply when he caught it under the front seat. Neither he nor Klett screamed, but otherwise the noise was terrible—rending, scraping, tearing—and still they fell. How far away was the ground?

Simon's Uncle Morris would be so disappointed that he'd forgotten the words to the Kaddish.

SIMON REGAINED CONSCIOUSNESS AT dusk. He was still strapped into his seat in the tail section of the plane, but cold, dark, empty space yawned in front of him. The rest of the airplane was missing. In the dim light he spotted it about twenty feet ahead, wings gone, the cockpit crumpled into the base of a broad oak. There was no fire, thank God. All he could think of was getting to Klett. He struggled with his seat belt, finally untangling himself. His ankle was too painful to stand on, so he crawled on hands and knees across hard, rocky ground toward the nose of the airplane.

Klett was dead, his corpse wedged so tightly between the dash and his seat that Simon couldn't budge him. What had been the instrument panel was a morass of broken glass, smashed dials, and dangling wires. The radio was demolished, crushed by the engine, which extruded part of the way into the passenger seat. Simon turned away from the wreck, sank to the cold ground outside the plane, and vomited. Or he would have if he'd eaten anything since the morning. He couldn't stop shaking.

Simon crawled back to the tail of the airplane, pulled himself up onto the back seats, and reached into the rear space where the fuel cans had been stored. He'd seen a cheap plastic tote back there, and he prayed it contained supplies of some kind.

The bag held minimal survival gear. A musty army blanket, which Simon draped over his shoulders, two bottles of water, four energy bars past their sell-by date, a roll of duct tape, and a box of matches sealed in a plastic sandwich bag. No flashlight, no space blanket, no radio, no flares, no freeze-dried meals, no camp stove. Simon had a dull pocketknife that he carried for sentimental reasons—his father had it given to him   a useless cell phone, and a packet of aspirin.

Simon knew he had to treat his shock and survive the night if he had any hope of living. He wrapped the army blanket around himself and lay flat on his back on the seats with his legs and feet raised above his heart, feet propped on the seat back, to stabilize his blood pressure. He drank one of the bottles of water to hydrate himself.

When he awoke hours later in the dead of night, with a painful urge to urinate, he didn't know if he'd been unconscious or asleep. It was pitch-black and night sounds filled the air. He unfolded himself from his cramped position. He stood outside the airplane and sprayed urine in a semicircle in front of him, all around the open gap in the tail of the plane. Black bears were more interested in eating cookies and potato chips than people, but he remembered the Forest Service recently reintroduced red wolves to the park. The smell of his urine should keep all wildlife away.

Simon crawled back onto the airplane seats and wrapped the army blanket around him again. Where exactly was he? How far had they drifted from their flight path before they crashed? Was the impact beacon working? He knew his cell phone wouldn't work deep in these mountains, but he flicked it on automatically, just to make sure. No signal, of course.

All Simon knew was that he was somewhere in the eastern part of the Nantahala National Forest, over half a million acres, much of which was wilderness. "Nantahala" was an Indian word that meant "land of the noonday sun." Dawn came late in the deep gorges and valleys of the park because the sun had to rise above the tree line and ridges as well as the horizon.

Simon's jacket and blanket kept him fairly warm inside the skin of the rear half of the airplane, but it was October, and a cold front could blow in anytime. He guessed he was no more than four thousand feet above sea level, or he'd be much colder than he was.

Despite his bookish bent, Simon had been raised a country boy. He recalled the mantra offered up by veterans of the mountains—shelter, fire, water. Never in his wildest dreams had he ever imagined that he would use the survival information he learned at Boy Scout camp. The tail end of the airplane would make a good shelter, especially if he insulated it further with thick evergreen branches. Thank God he had matches. When the sun did rise, his first order of business would be to build a fire, for signaling as much as warmth, then to find water. He'd drunk one bottle of water and had one left. He would refill the empty bottle if he could find a source. Eighty inches of rain drenched the Appalachian Mountains each year, there were streams and springs and waterfalls everywhere. He just needed to get lucky and find one nearby. Leaving the crash site would be foolish in the extreme. He wasn't optimistic that the impact beacon was working, having seen the state of the cockpit, but the wreckage might be visible from the air. With satellite surveillance what it was today, a signal fire, coupled with visible wreckage, was his best hope of being rescued.

Then Simon thought of Klett, but he ruthlessly suppressed the wave of dismay that threatened to overwhelm him. Klett had been a good man, his death was a tragedy, but there was nothing he could do for him now. He had to focus on his own survival. He'd rage over Klett's death later.

Simon curled up on the airplane seat and tried to sleep. Mostly he worried.

The sun rose above the tree line about nine o'clock the next morning, which meant the airplane had crashed on a ridge and not in a holler. Simon's neck was stiff and sore, he couldn't move it easily. Black bruises spotted most of his body, the worst in a broad swath across his chest where his shoulder harness had caught him as the airplane fell. He gingerly felt his ribs. They were very painful, but he couldn't tell if he had any fractures. He stood on his bad ankle, testing it. It still hurt, but he could walk on it, so it must not be broken. He wrapped it in duct tape for support. He wasn't planning any hikes—leaving the vicinity of the airplane would be stupid—but he needed to be able to get around. He took a couple of aspirin with a swig of water. With his pocketknife he slit an opening in the middle of the blanket so he could wear it like a poncho. He had eaten one energy bar since the crash, and had three left. He ate a second one. He would be very hungry before this was over. Human beings could safely eat just about anything that crawled, swam, walked, or flew, but he fervently hoped he'd be rescued before he resorted to harvesting the native flora and fauna.

Simon crawled outside the wreck and oriented himself. He had been correct: the plane had crashed on a ridge, in a stand of old growth hardwoods with a few tall pines scattered among them. Rhododendron and laurel filled the undergrowth. Moss layered with a kaleidoscope of fallen fall leaves cushioned the forest floor. The fog that gave the Smoky Mountains their name swirled around his feet and collected in nooks and crannies. Until it burned off around noon, Simon would feel as if he were walking through a cloud.

Looking up at the carnage of broken branches created by the plunging airplane among the treetops, Simon gathered that the plane had broken in two when it hit a thick oak, breaking the mighty trunk of the tree itself in half. The nose end of the airplane, the heaviest, had concertinaed into the base of yet another tree, crushing Klett between the engine and the seat back. The tail end, with Simon still buckled into his seat, had landed in the undergrowth of rhododendron and laurel, cushioning the impact. The path of the crashing plane opened a gap in the canopy through which sunlight beamed onto the ground in a welcome circle in front of his shelter. The clearing would make it easier for searchers to see his fire and the wreckage of the airplane.

Simon needed to start a fire now. If he kept it burning continuously, surely someone would come looking for him, even if the impact beacon wasn't working.

He decided to haul as much wood as possible near the plane while he still had some energy. There was plenty of wood scattered about, including leafy branches knocked to the floor of the forest by the plane crash, and he dragged log after log of it over to the tail end of the plane.

He scooped up armfuls of pine straw, which made excellent tinder, and stuffed it inside the compartment to keep it dry and insulate it. He stacked the leafy branches he'd collected around the outside of the compartment to insulate it further. His shoulder and neck and ankle screamed in pain, but he worked through it. He lit a small fire, one that created enough smoke, he thought, to be seen, but not large enough to use too much wood. He didn't need it for warmth yet. By the time he was done he shook with exertion, sweat dripping under his clothes and blanket. He drank half of the rest of his water.

After a brief rest Simon limped in circles around his shelter, never letting it out of his sight, looking for water, watching his step among the rocks and stumps and logs. He didn't need to fall and break a leg or an arm. Simon didn't locate a stream or a spring, but he did find a rotted stump, colonized by mosses and liverwort, a natural reservoir filled with gallons of stagnant rainwater. It was sure to be flavored with the corpses of insects and tadpoles, the saliva of squirrels and raccoons, but he was happy to share it with them. He splashed water onto his face, cupped some in his hands, and drank it down. It tasted musty and raw. He drank all the water he could hold from the stump and then filled the empty liter bottle and took it back to his pitiful shelter.

Simon added more logs to his fire until the stream of smoke satisfied him that it would be visible. Visible, that is, if the clouds lifted. Ominous gray thunderclouds had been massing all morning, and now formed an impenetrable canopy overhead. He could sense a cold front coming, the barometer dropping. If it rained, keeping himself and the wood he'd collected dry was critical. Simon collected brush, any branches with leaves or needles still on them, pulling up smaller bushes by the roots, to shield his wood from rain. He stowed as many of the shorter logs as he could in the back of the plane behind the seat, then he layered brush over the gap in his shelter and crawled underneath it, just as raindrops began to fall. Inside, he was completely dry and fairly warm.

It could rain for days. This was a temperate rain forest, for God's sake. No one could spot him from the air, or from a fire tower, or even from an observation satellite if his crash site was hidden by clouds.

Simon assumed mountain search and rescue were looking for him. Klett had radioed Atlanta Center their last position. When they didn't arrive in Bryson City, Brenda Lambert would have notified the appropriate authorities. The trouble was, the plane had likely drifted beyond its last radio position in a wilderness area. Once he was located, a helicopter couldn't land in this terrain. His rescuers would have to travel overland to reach him.

The truth was, Simon didn't think the plane's impact beacon was working, or he would have heard a search aircraft overhead by now.

Now that he'd stopped moving around, Simon was in pain again. Who knew bruises and sprains could hurt so much? He took three more aspirins with a slug of water from the fresh bottle. He'd allow the water he'd gotten from the stump to settle in its bottle before he drank it. That wouldn't purify it, but at least it wouldn't be gritty.

He watched the rain patter through the gaps in his shelter. He'd give anything for a book, a newspaper, even a pad of paper to pass the time with, to distract him from the gnawing in his stomach. For a while he played a shell game with a pebble and three walnut shells. He won, of course, because he knew where the pebble was hidden. Most cultures had invented versions of shell games, as did the American Indian. As a child Simon often played an elderly Cherokee at a senior center his mother often visited in her job as a public health nurse. He lost every game. Somehow the pebble was never where he expected it to be. Finally he gave in to his hunger and ate another energy bar.

Primitive man, in the shelter of a toasty rock cave on days like this, would pass the time shaping points and scrapers, sewing hides, stringing beads on strands of bear gut, maybe painting a buffalo or two on the rock wall, signing it with a handprint. He'd have dried meat to keep his hunger pains away.

During the Clovis era man spent hours knapping spear points eighteen inches long, large enough to fell mammoths and giant elk. For just a thousand years man lived in North America alongside saber-toothed tigers, cave bears, mammoths with huge tusks, and giant ground sloths. Within that thousand years the megafauna became extinct, probably because of man's hunting prowess with those same Clovis points. After the big animals were gone, stone points evolved into much smaller spearheads and arrowheads, all that was needed to hunt bison and deer successfully. Simon wondered if Clovis man noticed that the big animals were disappearing on his watch, and what he thought about it.

Simon slept for a couple of hours, woke up, and saw rain still pouring down outside his shelter. He lay flat on his back on the seats and propped his feet up on the thin wall of what was left of Klett's beloved airplane.

Simon had heard that a person could survive for days without food, but he'd didn't see how. He daydreamed for a while about his aunt's Thanksgiving dinners, the turkey and ham, whipped sweet potatoes, mounds of green beans, yeast rolls and butter, apple and pumpkin pies.

The rain slowed and then stopped. Simon left his shelter, pushing aside the branches that covered the opening, and rebuilt his fire with dry wood. He propped a sheet of metal, torn off from the plane during the crash, behind the fire, to reflect heat back toward his shelter. Recklessly he added more logs to the fire, letting it flame up, needing the cheer it offered as much as its warmth. Clouds still crowded what sky showed through the treetops. Simon doubted the smoke of his fire could be seen.

Rain brought worms to the surface of the ground, and before long Simon had a handful of fat ones. He dropped them into one of the water bottles, where instinctively they'd purge themselves, then ate them raw, one at a time. Their pure protein would keep his stomach feeling full for hours.

In the late afternoon it grew dark. The last thing Simon did before retiring to his shelter was turn over a flat rock and harvest several grubs, fat white beetle larvae, each waving six chubby legs, which he toasted on a stick over his fire. He ate them without any revulsion.

11

Wait until I have finished my problem.
—ARCHIMEDES (D. 212 BC), GREEK MATHEMATICIAN,
ON BEING ORDERED BY A ROMAN SOLDIER TO
FOLLOW HIM TO HIS EXECUTION

LATER THAT NIGHT A COLD FRONT FOLLOWED ON THE HEELS of the thunderstorm, and the temperature plunged. Simon huddled inside his shelter wrapped up in his blanket. Whenever he fooled himself that he was warm and comfortable and dozed off, the fire died down, and he jerked awake, chilled by a blast of cold air seeping through a crevice somewhere, and he'd go outside to build up the fire again, exhaling vapor, stamping his feet, or rather his single uninjured foot, while he piled more logs on the fire.

About three in the morning, when Simon checked the night sky through the gap in the canopy, he saw a few stars twinkling. The sky had cleared. He mounded wood on the fire, letting the flames roar higher and higher. Its crackling and sparking cheered him, raising his hopes someone would rescue him soon.

When it was light enough for him to find his way

around the wreckage, Simon went back to the nose half of the airplane, still avoiding Klett's body, and twisted off one of the side mirrors. When the sun rose higher he would start signaling. He scanned the ground as he walked back to his shelter, batting away the fog swirling around his ankles, looking for something in the plant family to eat so he could avoid a worm and grub breakfast. There were plenty of mushrooms, but he didn't trust himself to distinguish the edible from the poisonous varieties. He hoped for dandelions or wild leeks, but couldn't find any. Instead he filled his pockets with hickory nuts and walnuts.

As he bent over again a small shiny rock gleamed at him from under a leaf, and he picked it up. It was an arrowhead, skillfully knapped from light gray rhyolite, a glassy form of quartz, the best rock available for making stone tools when flint wasn't available.

Finding the rhyolite arrowhead jogged Simon's memory. He remembered that Klett had told him about the scarcity of flint in North Carolina, that Mabry thought the flint Uwharrie Man used to work his point might have come from South Carolina or Virginia. And Morgan had been researching ore provenance in the early morning hours before his murder.

Simon stood rooted, staring at the arrowhead in his hand. He made a huge instinctive leap from musing over the arrowhead to the puzzle of Morgan's murder, considering a motive for the killing so twisted it hadn't crossed his mind before. At any rate, he had to survive before he concerned himself with Morgan's murder again. He tucked the arrowhead inside his jacket pocket.

He went back to his shelter, piled more wood on the fire, and ate his last energy bar. By now the sun was up, he felt warmer even if he wasn't, and he sat by the fire, focusing his mirror on the sun, trying to catch enough sunlight in the mirror to reflect a beam or two into the sky. Probably he succeeded just in blinding a few hawks, but it was something positive to do. After a time he got bored and cold and hungry, and went scrounging for more wood and something edible.

A couple of hours before dusk, while dining on a potage of mashed sassafras roots, ramps, and nuts, Simon heard an engine. He jumped to his feet, piled more wood on the fire, and hollered. It was the first time he'd used his voice since the crash, and the sound of it echoed unfamiliarly around him.

A hefty all-terrain vehicle, with tires the size of tractors, driven by a man in a Forest Service uniform, emerged from the trees.

The ranger got off his vehicle and pulled off his helmet. From his high cheekbones and jet-black hair Simon guessed he was Cherokee.

"Where the hell have you been?" Simon said. "I pay taxes, you know."

"Not enough," the ranger said, grinning at him and grasping Simon's outstretched hand. "We've got fifty thousand acres in this district. We just got satellite photos this morning. What with lightning strikes, fog, and thunderstorm damage, there were a dozen likely locations for us to scout."

"I'm Simon Shaw."

"I'm Ed Simmons. Where's the other guy?"

Simon nodded over toward the wrecked nose of the airplane. Without warning his throat closed and his voice broke. "Henry Klett," Simon said. "He died."

"I'm so sorry," the ranger said. "It's a wonder you survived. It was twelve degrees last night. Here," he said, pulling an insulated Forest Service jacket out of a pack behind the seat of the ATV, "put this on. Water?" He handed Simon a liter bottle of clear, clean, non-critter-flavored water.

Simon discarded the filthy blanket and reeking jacket he'd been wearing since the crash and shoved his arms into the sleeves of the thick coat, pulling the hood over his head. Then he tipped back the bottle of water and drained it. Meanwhile, the ranger went over to the wrecked nose of the airplane, peered through the window, and shook his head.

"Too damn bad," he said, walking back to Simon. "You want something to eat?" he asked. "I've got ham sandwiches."

The two of them sat on the ground next to the fire while Simon gulped down a sandwich. His hands were dirty, the camp was damp and cold, his shelter not even as advanced as a hut. He'd been living like his prehistoric ancestors for a couple of days, and he'd never forget the experience as long as he lived.

Forget Winston Churchill and Albert Einstein. From now on Simon's heroes were the men who'd perfected hunting, the women who'd discovered how to harvest grain and make bread, the clans of early humans who learned to work together and so invent civilization.

The ranger studied Simon's shelter.

"How did you know to do this?" he asked.

"Boy Scout camp," Simon said. "My parents made me go. I hated it."

"Got any idea what happened to the airplane?" the ranger asked.

"Klett said the fuel wasn't getting to the engine," Simon said.

"You're sure the tanks were full? You'd be surprised how many private plane pilots run out of gas."

"He checked them both before we left the airport."

"Visually?"

"Yeah. We had gas. Of course, when it became clear we were going to crash he jettisoned it. One thing . . ."

"What?"

"He said, that if I lived"—here Simon had to control his voice again—"I should make sure that the FAA checked out the fuel tanks. He said something wasn't right."

"You're implying that someone sabotaged the tanks? Who would do that?"

Simon explained that Klett was a member of a committee charged with a decision that might ruin careers, and that another committee member had been murdered several days ago.

"You on the same committee?"

"No," Simon said, shaking his head. "But the murder victim was a good friend of mine. Are we going to be able to take Dr. Klett's body with us?"

"No," the ranger said. "We'll have to send a recovery team back here, with the FAA investigators. I've got a GPS device with me. I'll get the coordinates, and first place we get to where my satellite phone will work, I'll phone them in. And let your family know you're okay."

And let Klett's know he was dead.

"Let's make sure your fire is extinguished," the ranger said. He pulled a folding shovel from a pack on the back on the ATV and dumped shovelfuls of dirt on the fire.

While Simmons shoveled, Simon scanned the crash site, committing the scene to memory. The broken, crumpled airplane, the piles of wood stacked next to his fire, the tail of the airplane stuffed with brush and covered with branches for insulation, the rotting hollow stump filled with stagnant rainwater that had sustained his life, the cold, damp layer of fall leaves and emerald moss that carpeted the forest floor, and the tall straight pines and oaks that blotted out most of the sun. Then he climbed on to the back of the ATV behind the ranger.

The two men jolted their way across the ridge and down into a holler, which they followed for miles, rambling around fallen trees, climbing over outcrops of rock, and fording several shallow streams until they reached a well-worn animal track zigzagging down the mountain. A few miles farther along they stopped at a clearing, where the ranger found Simon another bottle of water, checked his GPS device, and used his satellite telephone. After he finished his conversation, he remounted the ATV.

"Its just a few miles from here to the road where I left the truck," he said. "I've let the sheriff's office in Sylva know you're okay."

The track was smooth enough that Simon dozed off with his arms around the ranger's waist and his head on his shoulder. When the ATV stopped and he woke up, he saw that they'd halted on a wide gravel road. A Forest Service flatbed truck was parked with its ramp down on the shoulder of the road.

"Here," the ranger said, "you get in the truck. There's a Thermos of coffee on the seat. I think there's some left. Let me load up the ATV and we'll be on our way."

He drove the ATV up the ramp and closed the tailgate. Just before he got in the truck his satellite phone rang. He walked a few feet away from the truck before answering it.

When he'd finished his conversation, he got into the driver's seat of the truck and started the engine.

"Any coffee left?" he asked.

"No, sorry," Simon said.

"No problem. You need it more than me," he said. "That was the sheriff of Jackson County. He said that your cousin is going to meet you in Sylva, at the sheriff's office. He wanted to know if you want to hold a press conference."

"Hell, no." Simon said.

"Private plane crashes are big news around here," he said. "Survivors are even bigger."

"No way, no reporters," Simon said. "Tell them I'm going to an undisclosed location to recuperate."

"Do you think you need to go to the emergency room?"

"If I do, I'll get my cousin to take me," Simon said. "I don't want any fuss."

The ranger used the truck radio to tell the sheriff in Sylva that Simon wanted no press, no ambulance, no welcoming committee, no drama of any kind when he returned to civilization.

It was dark by the time they arrived in Cullowhee, a pretty town tucked into the side of a mountain. At a convenience store the ranger handed Simon over to a sheriff's deputy for a lift to Sylva, the county seat. Simon shook his rescuer's hand.

"Thanks," Simon said to the ranger. "This sounds stupid, but if I can ever do anything for you . . ."

"Just keep paying those taxes."

The deputy sheriff who drove him to Sylva was a quiet man who preferred to listen to country music rather than talk. Despite the coffee he'd had, Simon dozed off again.

THE JACKSON COUNTY GOVERNMENT center in Sylva was a modern four-story building built of local gray stone. Tall floodlights lit the entrance to the sheriff's office, where the sheriff himself and a deputy met them.

Sheriff Delbert Owen shook his hand.

"Thanks for getting rid of the reporters," Simon said.

"Not a problem," Sheriff Owen said. "I told them you were going to the emergency room in Cherokee for a checkup. That should distract them for a couple hours."

"Your cousin should be here any minute," the deputy said. She was a solid young woman with a brown ponytail and teased bangs piled around her face. "How about something to eat while you wait?"

"I'd rather have a shower, if that's possible," Simon said.

"Sure," the sheriff said. "Come on in here. We got a shower in the intake room where we make the prisoners clean up after they're arrested. We can give you clean clothes and underwear, too."

Suddenly Simon didn't think he could wait even a minute to get clean.

"Yes, please," Simon said.

"Let me find you an inmate toilet kit. The soap in it will take the top layer of your skin off."

"I hope there's a toothbrush, too. I've been eating grubs and ramps."

Simon stood in the concrete shower stall, which was open to the prisoner intake room, with his face lifted to the showerhead, steaming-hot water streaming over him.

"Want me to throw this away?" the sheriff said, pointing to the heap of filthy clothes Simon had discarded.

"Yeah," Simon said. "Except for my wallet and stuff, and there's an arrowhead in a pocket somewhere. Hang on to that, too."

"Deputy," the sheriff called out into the hall, "we need a jumpsuit and underwear in here, everything extra small."

Simon scrubbed himself twice, got out of the shower, and found that the sheriff had left the room to give him some privacy. He brushed his teeth. Toothpaste never tasted so good. The sheriff had placed the arrowhead, his wallet, cell phone, and pocketknife on top of a pile of jail clothing. Simon changed into the worn underwear and olive drab jumpsuit and rubber shoes. The adrenaline that had sustained him for the last two days continued its slow leak out of his body. He stumbled out of the intake room, where the sheriff took his elbow and guided him into a cell and onto a cot.

Simon's cousin Luther Coffey dragged him off the cot and enveloped him in a bear hug.

"Thank you, Jesus!" Luther said. "Thank you!"

"Hey, Luther," Simon said, yawning.

"Let me look at you, you puny bastard! I am so damn glad to see you!"

"I'm happy to see you, too."

"You look like you been arrested."

"My clothes were filthy."

Luther held him out at arm's length.

"You could look worse. How did you manage? It was cold as a witch's tit out last night."

"Remember when we learned all that survival stuff at Boy Scout camp? And I was lucky I wasn't seriously injured in the crash."

"I always heard the back of a plane is the safest place to be."

Luther sat next to him on the cot. Simon and Luther were the same age, first cousins, but didn't resemble each other at all. In looks Luther took after Simon's father's side of the family. He was built burly, like a bear, carrying more muscle than fat despite all the beer and barbecue he consumed. He wore what he would consider church clothes, khaki trousers, a white shirt, polished cowboy boots, a corduroy jacket with a leather collar, and a ball cap with an Appalachian State logo shoved over his fading ginger hair.

"What happened?" Luther asked. "I know the pilot died. I waited with his family in Cherokee. Nice people, real broken up, as you can imagine. They left after we got the word."

"Klett said that gas wasn't getting to the tanks even though they were full. I don't think we'll know anything else until after the FAA investigates."

"I got a room in a good motel in Cherokee. You feel like going on over there, or do you want to stay here? You hurt at all? Need to see a doctor?"

"Sprained my ankle, that's all, but yeah, I want to go on to the hotel, sleep in a real bed."

"Good. I'm tired. I've had a rough couple of days."

Simon said his thanks and goodbyes to the sheriff and his deputy.

"I guess you couldn't let me know what the FAA inspector thinks about the plane crash, could you?" he asked the sheriff.

" 'Fraid not," Sheriff Owen said. "But the official report is public information. It'll be a few weeks before that's out."

Simon went through his wallet and extracted Otis Gates's business card.

"How about a Raleigh police sergeant?" he asked. "Otis Gates. He's on the homicide case I told you about."

"Yeah," the sheriff said. "Yeah. I could talk to him about it."

Luther's truck waited outside. It was new, an immense double cab pickup, black with a gold iridescent lightning bolt streaking down its side. Its tires looked like they belonged on a bulldozer used for building roads in the Andes. The truck stood so high off the ground Simon had to pull himself up to get in it.

"What are you planning to do with this thing, subjugate Fallujah?" Simon asked.

"You're just jealous you ain't got one," Luther said. "Get on in the back seat and get some sleep."

"YOUR VOICE IS ECHOING oddly," Marcus said.

"I'm in the bathtub," Simon said. "Testing the hot water heater. Want to see how many times I can fill up the tub before the hot water runs out."

"Take care of yourself. Let us know when you're home."

"I will."

Simon clicked off his cell phone and tossed it onto the pile of towels on the floor. With his big toe he turned the spigot and dribbled more hot water into the tub, then submerged himself up to his nose. He felt okay, considering his ordeal. His ankle still ached, but he could walk on it.

The door to the motel room slammed open and Luther entered with supplies. Simon stayed in the tub while he unwrapped his egg and bacon biscuit and doctored his extra-large coffee with cream and sugar. Luther lowered the toilet seat and piled a stack of new clothes on it. He tipped toiletries out of a drugstore bag on the counter.

"I believe I got everything you requested," Luther said, "except, darn it, I forgot the bubble bath."

Simon ignored him, concentrating on his breakfast.

"You should let me take you to the emergency room," Luther said. "Those bruises look like sunset before a hurricane."

"I'm fine," Simon said. "I just want to get home."

"Momma said I was to bring you up to Boone with me for a few days. She wants to feed you up."

"I appreciate the thought, Luther, but I've got unfinished business at home. Papers to grade, midterms coming up. I just want to put this behind me."

Luther shook his head at Simon.

"I'll come home for Thanksgiving, I promise," Simon said.

Simon transferred his stuff, including the arrowhead, from his county jail clothes to the pockets of the jeans

Luther had brought him. He tossed the arrowhead in his hand a couple of times before tucking it away, thinking about how to proceed with his suspicions. He wondered if Denise was in jail in Raleigh yet, and if Otis would accept a telephone call from him. He regretted the angry words they'd exchanged.

Simon got Otis's voice mail at his office.

"It's me," he said to the machine. "I wanted to apologize—"

Otis picked up the telephone. "I'm the one who should apologize," he said. "I'm glad you're not dead. I hated to think our last conversation was an argument."

"Me, too," Simon said. "I was in the wrong."

"Maybe not."

"What do you mean?"

"Denise McGrath's been cleared."

Simon felt an enormous weight lifted from him. His dear friend had not died by his own sister's hand. It had been worth surviving the plane crash to learn this.

"She proved she was at the conference?" Simon asked.

"Not hardly," Otis said. "The Knoxville police were at her home to arrest her, they actually had handcuffs on her, when she burst into tears and finally told them the truth."

"Which was?"

"She and a male colleague skipped out on the teachers' conference and went off together. They were at an inn at Myrtle Beach. That's why she had all those miles on her car. She didn't want her husband to find out, of course."

"Her husband's disabled," Simon said. "Her life's been pretty rough for the last few years."

"So I understand. According to the Knoxville detective who talked to her, she just wanted to get away from everything for a few days. The guy she went with, and the staff at the inn, confirmed her story."

"Now what?"

"I don't know," Otis said. "You know as well as I do that unless a murder is solved within forty-eight hours it's likely to stay unsolved. It's been over a week since Dr. Morgan was killed. I'm back to considering the hapless burglar or your theory that involves that skeleton committee."

"Listen to this," Simon said. He told Otis that Klett suspected that his airplane had been sabotaged, and that an FAA team was on its way to the crash site. He also told him that Sheriff Owen had promised to call Gates with the FAA team's first impressions of the cause of the crash.

"Klett was working on a compromise over the skeleton," Simon said, explaining in detail the conversation between Henry Klett and Lowery.

"Could Brad Lowery have sabotaged the plane?"

"He drove us to the airport in Lumberton. He was alone with the airplane while Klett and I used the bathroom."

"I'll question Lowery first thing, and I'll call the Jackson County sheriff tomorrow if I don't hear from him today," Otis said.

"Otis," Simon said, "what happened when you talked to Martha Dunn?"

"Oh, yeah. That's one angry young woman. You can cross her name out of your little black book. She seemed to think you should have talked to her before reporting her to the police. She had a receipt from a flea market booth for the Indian artifacts, and said she didn't intend to search your office, that it occurred to her just when she woke up in the middle of the night."

"She would say that, though." Martha would hardly

admit that she'd slept with Simon to get access to his office. Or, as Simon hated to think, that Mabry had put her up to it.

"Simon," Otis said, "I know I was wrong about Denise McGrath, but I still want you to stay out of this. Someone may have murdered Klett. You could be a target, too, if the killer thinks you know too much."

"I've thought about that myself," Simon said. "I'm going to stay with my family in Boone for a while."

Luther stopped stuffing his clothes into his duffel and raised an eyebrow at Simon.

"Good. I'll keep you up to speed," Otis said.

Simon clicked off his cell phone.

"I thought you were going back to your place," Luther said.

"I am, but I don't want anyone to know I'm there," Simon said.

Luther finished packing while Simon strapped on an ankle support Luther had gotten him at the drugstore. He stood on the ankle. The ankle still hurt, but he'd be able to walk as much as he needed to.

Simon stopped in the motel lobby and answered questions from the reporters who'd camped out there hoping for a human interest story. No, he had no idea at all why the airplane had crashed; yes, he was going to Boone to recuperate; no, he wouldn't consent to any more interviews.

Simon and Luther drove through Cherokee on their way out of town to pick up the Blue Ridge Parkway. Cherokee, the capital of the eastern band of the Cherokee nation, sat on both banks of the Oconaluftee, a wide, rocky river that cut through the Qualla Boundary. The river was stocked with trout, and even in the middle of town Simon could see people fishing, wearing waders, standing up to their waists in frothy water. As they drove farther through town, they passed the Qualla Arts and Crafts Mutual, the tribal council house, and the Museum of the Cherokee.

Simon thought he knew a lot about the Cherokee just from growing up in western North Carolina, until his colleague Jack Kingfisher explained the evolution of the eastern band of the Cherokee to him. The eastern band evolved from one Cherokee community, the Oconaluftee, who escaped removal to Oklahoma by withdrawing from the Cherokee nation rather than agreeing to the treaty that exchanged their lands for a reservation in Oklahoma. The federal authorities couldn't budge them from their mountains, so finally the U.S. government recognized the Qualla Boundary, which was land these Cherokee actually bought for themselves, as an eastern Cherokee reservation. The eastern band survived by any means they could, selling timber, farming, even dressing as plains Indians in feather headdresses to lure a thriving tourist trade. Souvenir shops, an outdoor drama, and magnificent scenery still drew visitors, but the tribe's newest venture, an enormous Harrah's Casino, promised real prosperity. Once the casino began to make money, plenty of North Carolinians searched their family history for that Indian relative who might supply the one-sixteenth Cherokee ancestry that would entitle them to a cut from the casino profits.

Simon and Luther drove out of town, exiting off Highway 19 past the casino, and cruised the Blue Ridge Parkway north until they reached Asheville. There they left the parkway and found a budget car rental agency, where Simon rented an inconspicuous sedan.

"I'm not sure about this," Luther said. "I wish you'd wait a couple days."

"I can't. Remember, tell Aunt Rae it's important, real important, that she pretend I'm at her house resting from my ordeal. Okay? I don't want anyone to have a clue I'm in Raleigh, even Otis."

Luther headed north to Boone, while Simon got on Interstate 40 for the five-hour drive home to Raleigh. Five hours was more than enough time for him to get good and scared. Two men had been murdered, for he didn't doubt that Klett's airplane had been sabotaged, and he feared that they wouldn't be the last.

As he drove Simon couldn't take his mind off the rhyolite arrowhead in his back pocket. When he'd picked it up from the damp ground it had sparked an intuitive train of thought that led in his mind straight to a motive for Morgan's murder. What was that Seneca quote? "He who profits by villainy, has perpetrated it." But motive was useless without hard facts to corroborate it.

Certainly Otis wouldn't be impressed by his intuitive speculations; that's why he didn't mention his suspicions to him. He was going home unannounced so he could avoid the attentions of his friends and focus on finding the evidence he needed to lock up a murderer for life.

12

SMALL BOY: Where do animals go when they die?
SMALL GIRL: All good animals go to heaven, but the bad
ones go to the Natural History Museum.
—CAPTION TO A DRAWING BY E. H. SHEPARD, *PUNCH,* 1929

SIMON DROVE BY HIS HOUSE. HIS THUNDERBIRD SAT UNDER
the carport. Someone must have picked it up in Lumberton and driven it home for him. He wanted badly to pull
into his own driveway, walk through his own door, sleep
tonight in his own bed, but he passed on by his house.

In the few days he'd been gone the city had costumed
itself for Halloween, briefly overwhelming autumn displays
of mums and pumpkins and obnoxiously early Christmas decorations. Paper ghosts roosted in trees, jack-o'-
lanterns grinned from porches and steps, and black cats
pranced across front yards. This year Hanukkah fell on
Christmas Eve, so silver and blue Stars of David and
menorahs made their token appearances in store windows. Whatever happened to Thanksgiving, his favorite
holiday? For years he'd stubbornly refused to start pre-

paring for Christmas until December first, but he was losing that battle.

Simon drove downtown to what Raleigh residents called the round hotel, a twenty-story, circular, midcentury landmark with a restaurant on the top floor. Built as a Holiday Inn, it was now operated by one of those generic motel companies. As he drove along Hillsborough Street the Christmas lights bloomed with colored auras, Halloween ghosts and goblins seemed to lunge out at him from the yards he passed. He was disoriented and exhausted. He needed to eat something, but he was too tired to stop. When he parked in the motel lot he narrowly missed sideswiping another car.

In his hotel room, Simon emptied his pockets, took off his jacket, shook off his shoes, and got under the covers fully dressed. He fell asleep immediately.

SIMON AWOKE THE NEXT morning after twelve hours' sleep feeling refreshed but very hungry. He didn't want to go to the restaurant in case someone he knew dropped in for breakfast, and there was no room service, so he called Danny.

"Yeah," the teenager answered the phone. "What is it?"

"Did I wake you up?" Simon asked.

"Yeah. Move over, you big baby. Not you, it's my dog."

"Sorry."

"Simon, is that you? Where are you?"

"I'm in town, but not at home."

"You okay? Man, I can't imagine being in a plane crash. You must be, like, seriously traumatized."

"I think it'll hit me later. I hope my insurance covers post-traumatic stress disorder. Listen, I don't want anyone to know I'm here. I've got some stuff to do, and I need help."

"Sure." Simon heard the mattress creak as the boy sat up.

"I'm down the street at the round hotel. Room two-sixteen. I need my laptop and some clothes. My laptop's in my study. There should be a CD right there on my desk marked *Morgan*. And a yellow pad full of Morgan's notes. Bring those, too. And food. I'm starving. And lots of coffee. Have you got enough money? I've got cash here."

"I can swing it. I'll be there in half an hour. I need to get dressed and let Luke out first."

SIMON HAD JUST GOTTEN out of the shower when Danny knocked at his hotel room door. He wrapped himself in a towel and let the boy in. Danny carried one of Simon's duffel bags and a fast-food bag smelling of bacon and coffee. The boy threw an arm around him and hugged him. Simon hugged him back, choking back a surge of emotion.

"I'm damn glad to see you," Simon said to him.

"Me, too. When I heard your plane went down, I thought I might be going to your funeral," Danny said. "Then who would I borrow money from?"

"Close the door and have a seat," Simon said. He quickly changed into fresh clothes while Danny unpacked egg and bacon biscuits, orange juice, and four large paper cups of coffee. He dumped envelopes of sugar and tiny cartons of cream out of the bag.

"One coffee for me, three for you," Danny said.

"I'm going to need them all."

After they'd eaten, Simon stuffed their trash back into the food bag. He doctored his second coffee with sugar and cream.

"Well," Danny said, "so what's going on? Why are you hiding out here?"

"I can't say," Simon said.

"Oh, come on!"

"No, not yet." Simon pulled a twenty-dollar bill out of his wallet and stuffed it in Danny's shirt pocket. "Food and gas," he said.

"Does this have something to do with Dr. Morgan's murder? And the plane crash? Give me a hint!"

"I have lots of ideas and no facts, yet, but I plan on finding those facts. I promise to tell you everything as soon as I can. Go on to school, okay?"

"Wakes me up at dawn," he said, "bring me food, he says, get me coffee." Danny tossed his book bag over his shoulder. "And what do I get in return? Nada, zilch."

"Get over it," Simon said. "And don't tell anyone I'm here."

Danny left, grumbling.

For the next two hours Simon drank coffee and went through Morgan's notes and the CD of the contents of his computer again. Simon believed he'd found a pattern in Morgan's research on Uwharrie Man. It was slight, very slight, confirmation of what had crossed his mind when he picked up that arrowhead in the mountains. Morgan wasn't an expert in early prehistory, and the sequence of Web sites he visited the night of his murder showed him educating himself. As he progressed from Web site to Web site, his research narrowed until it became very specific.

The last three Web sites he visited on the morning of his murder concerned stone tool chronologies and dating methodologies. He'd logged on to the last Web site at twelve past five in the morning, minutes before his death.

SIMON PULLED HIS RENTAL car into a space at the state fairgrounds, where the Raleigh flea market set up shop most days. Two buildings crammed with booths opened every day, while the parking lot filled up with tailgate vendors on the weekend.

He quickly located the only booth selling antiquities, four spaces down from the homemade fudge and next to the guy who wood-burned biblical verses onto pine plaques.

Simon leaned on the counter.

"Hey," he said.

"Hey yourself," the vendor said. He wasn't real old, just well worn, over sixty, with leathery skin and strong hands. He was bandy-legged in the jeans cinched to his skinny waist with a leather belt joined by a NASCAR buckle. Simon guessed he was a retired tobacco farmer. His booth was stocked with arrowheads, broken ceramics, colonial nails and hardware, and primitive wooden trenchers and bowls.

"You got anything good?" Simon asked.

"All this is authentic," the vendor said.

"I could go right outside and dig down a couple feet and find more of the same. I mean, do you have anything rare? You know what I'm saying."

"I got one special item today," he said. He bent over and pulled a box from under his counter. He opened it and pulled out an object cushioned in bubble wrap. Unwrapping it slowly and carefully to heighten the suspense, he revealed a prehistoric stone axe head.

"That's what I'm talking about," Simon said. He picked up the axe head. "Very nice." It was a beautiful object, expertly knapped, clearly showing striations where it had been secured to its wooden shaft with animal gut. "Not what I'm looking for, though."

"Tell me what you want. I might be able to find it for you."

"I'd like a Folsom blade."

He snorted. "Wouldn't we all," he said.

"A stone pipe would be nice. And two intact pots, one small, fabric-impressed, the other cord-marked."

The vendor's eyes narrowed. "Where did you hear about that lot?" he asked. "I sold it to a girl graduate student on condition she didn't say she got it from me."

"Where did it come from?"

"None of your business."

Simon put both hands on the counter and bent over it, leaning into the vendor's face.

"Don't mess with me," Simon said. "Unless you want me to turn you in for selling stolen antiquities."

"Weren't stolen. I collected them myself."

Simon leaned farther over the counter and grabbed the vendor by one wrist, twisting it hard.

"Hey! Let go of me! I'll holler out to the security guard!"

"You didn't collect those artifacts. They belonged to a friend of mine—"

"I swear—"

"Who was murdered."

"I know nothing about that, nothing!"

"I don't give a damn where you get the stuff you sell. I don't care if it's stolen. But I want to know where you got those four objects, and I want to know right now. You realize if you withhold information from the police, you could be charged as an accessory?"

"Okay, okay. Leave me out of this. I got all of it from a pothunter."

Simon released his hand, and the vendor stepped back from the counter, rubbing his wrist.

"Who?"

"I don't know his name. He brings me stuff regular. I always pay cash."

"When did you buy it?"

"Over a week ago, I don't remember exactly. The stuff was still on the counter when that girl grad student came by and she bought them right away."

"What did he look like? This supplier?"

"Medium size, not as old as me. He always wears dark glasses and a hat."

"That's it?"

"I got macular degeneration and a cataract that ain't ripe yet. I don't see that good."

"Give me a break."

"Really. Ask anybody around here. I can't even drive. My wife has to tote me."

SIMON SAT OUTSIDE THE flea market in his car and fretted. He should call Otis and tell him that the artifacts in Martha's apartment were Morgan's after all. He didn't know what use the information would be, though. He doubted the pothunter was Morgan's murderer. He probably received the goods from someone else, who could have gotten them from someone else yet again.

Simon's cell phone rang. It was Otis.

"Hey, Simon," Otis said. "How are you? Are your relatives driving you crazy?"

Simon couldn't lie to him outright again. Their friendship was on shaky ground as it was.

"I'm in Raleigh, Otis."

There was a brief pause.

"You fool," Otis said. "What is wrong with you?"

"No one knows I'm here. I'm staying at the round hotel."

"That's something. What the hell, I should have known you wouldn't stay away. But lie low. You were right, that plane crash was sabotage."

A flashback exploded out of the dark recesses of Simon's mind like a freight train roaring out of a tunnel, he heard Klett's strained voice, saw the ground coming up at them fast, heard the sound of grating, shredding metal as the airplane ripped through dozens of tree branches.

"You okay?"

"Yeah," Simon said.

"The FAA inspector said someone stuffed rags in both gas tanks," Otis said. "The rags slowly soaked up gasoline, floated around the tanks for a while, then sank all the way to the bottom of the tanks, finally blocking the gas outlet, starving the engines of fuel."

"What kind of rags?"

"The usual shop rags you'd find where engine work is being done. A Robeson County sheriff's deputy found a box at the Lumberton Airport. Lowery had plenty of time to stuff the tanks while you were in the bathroom."

"I'm afraid so."

"Brad Lowery had motive and opportunity for both murders. We still don't have any physical evidence to implicate him, though."

Simon told Otis about his encounter with the flea market vendor.

"I'll get on that, too. If we can track down the fence, maybe he can identify Lowery," Otis said.

"Seems odd Lowery would take such a chance," Simon said. "You'd think he'd just throw the stuff away."

"It's hard to pass up good money," Otis said. "Do me a favor, lie low until I tell you we've arrested Lowery. He might come after you next. Like I said, we need corroborating evidence before we can pick him up. We need witnesses who saw him on Morgan's street, the murder weapon, fingerprints on the airplane gas tank, otherwise all this is just speculation."

"Don't worry," Simon said. "I want to stay alive." Miserable as life was at times it beat the alternative.

After Otis hung up, Simon got out of his car and walked around the flea market, trying to settle the shakiness caused by his flashback.

After he'd walked up and down the aisles of booths selling homemade jams and jellies, handmade furniture, stained glass, and jewelry, his ankle started to hurt, so he bought a real lemonade, lemons squeezed and sugar mixed in a metal pitcher dripping with condensation, and went outside and sat on a bench under a tree. He didn't know what to do. He was tired. He wished he could just go home and go back to work. He took the arrowhead he'd picked up in the mountains out of his pocket and rolled it around in his hand.

SIMON ATE LUNCH AT the K & W Cafeteria, eating real food, fried chicken, okra, turnip greens, and biscuits, for the first time since the crash. While there he marshaled his thoughts about the murders, drinking coffee and nibbling at a piece of lemon meringue pie while scribbling notes on the journalist's pad he always carried with him.

He started with the premise that Morgan had been killed because of his opinion on the disposition of Uwharrie Man. Even Otis now thought this was likely. The killer must have known, perhaps from a conversation that morning, that Morgan was in favor of studying the skeleton. After he killed Morgan, the killer sedated the dogs, either to keep them quiet or to conceal the fact that they knew him. He then stole some of Morgan's artifacts and his wallet, hoping the murderer would look like a botched robbery. Simon assumed the murderer then searched for Morgan's notes, which he didn't find because Morgan had mislaid them at the library.

After Morgan's death, every member of the committee hounded Simon about those notes. When he finally did locate them, Klett, Mabry, and Dunn benefited from their contents. Klett used the knowledge of Morgan's opinion to propose a compromise wherein his museum would house the remains during their study, Mabry would get the glory of a groundbreaking find, and Martha could finish her dissertation. Lowery was the man left out in the cold. Under Klett's proposed compromise, all the Lumbee nation got was the opportunity to appoint a Native American anthropologist to the study and to acquire the skeleton after it was completed. Was that enough of a victory for Lowery?

MARTHA'S CAR WAS OUT in front of her apartment. Simon drove around the block a couple of times. This would be a difficult and nasty scene, but he had to confront her.

It was worse than he expected.

When Martha opened the door and saw him, her face flooded red with anger and embarrassment.

"You bastard," she said. "How dare you show up here!"

Simon shoved his foot over the frame of the door to prevent her from slamming it in his face.

"We need to talk," he said.

"Go to hell," she said, shoving the door hard against his foot, shooting pain from his damaged ankle up to his shin.

"Move, damn it!"

"Five minutes," Simon said. "That's all I ask."

She let go of the door, and Simon came into the apartment. Unfortunately, she let go of the door to go over to a bureau and pull out a snub-nosed revolver, pointing it right at him.

"It's loaded," she said.

"I'm sure it is," Simon said, closing the door behind him. "Put it down, please. You look ridiculous."

She slammed the gun back in the drawer.

"Where did you get that thing?" Simon asked.

"My daddy gave it to me when I moved into my first apartment."

"We need to talk."

"Get out, damn it!" Without her gun to wave around, Martha resorted to stamping a foot for effect.

"Five minutes," he said.

"It better be one hell of an apology."

"Apology? What apology? What do I have to apologize for?"

"How insensitive can you be? I come tripping home last Friday evening, ready to pack for a weekend with you, all atwitter with the promise of new love, and I find the police here! Waiting for me! Asking me questions like I was suspected of Dr. Morgan's murder! You turned me in! Don't you think you could have come to me first with your nasty suspicions? I could have explained the artifacts! I could have gone to the police myself!"

"You're not the only person who's bitter. I had to tell the police that you slept with me so you could search my office. How do you think that made me feel?"

"That's not what happened."

"You expect me to believe that? You were desperate to know if Morgan had indicated in his notes how he planned to vote. And you told me that Mabry thought I was deliberately hiding them."

Martha sank down on her sofa. Her blond hair hung in strings, she had circles under her eyes, and the shirt she wore over her worn blue jeans needed ironing.

She burst into tears.

Oh, no, Simon thought. Crying was such an unfair weapon in the battle between the sexes. It got him every time.

He sat down next to her and rubbed her back.

"I'm sorry," he said. "Really sorry. You're absolutely right, I should have talked to you first. It was a nasty thing to do. And when we went to dinner, I was just as interested in questioning you as you were in quizzing me."

She dried her eyes with the hem of her shirt.

"It's true," she said, "I did have ulterior motives for going out with you, but what happened later, that evening, that was genuine. The thing is, I woke up in the middle of the night, and I started thinking about what would happen if I couldn't write this dissertation. I can't afford to start over again. I just can't. So I went into your office and poked around. It was reprehensible behavior, I know. I'm so ashamed of myself."

"I can tell you don't make a habit of it. You left signs you'd been in there one of my cats could read."

She leaned into him. She was so pretty, even in her disheveled state, with tear tracks down her face.

"I don't know what got into me," she said. "I don't usually behave like this."

"Me neither. It's been a stressful time."

"Tell me it's not over between us," she said.

"We've both made mistakes, and we both regret them," Simon said. "I think we could start again. I'd like to try."

He took her in his arms and kissed her. She climbed into his lap, wrapped her arms around him, one hand splayed across his back, the other reaching inside his jeans.

Simon gently disentangled her.

"What's wrong?" she asked. "Aren't we making up?"

"Later," Simon said. "There's something the two of us need to do first. There's more at stake here than your dissertation."

"That's easy for you to say. You've got your job, your tenure, your first book behind you. Just thinking about it makes me want a drink."

"I hope you've got enough for me."

Martha went into her kitchen and located the bourbon, pouring them each a stiff drink. After Simon finished his, he set the empty glass on the table.

"I need you to hear me out," he said.

"Okay, about what?"

"First," he said, pointing at the little cluster of objects on her bookcase, "those are Morgan's artifacts, the ones stolen from his office."

"No, they're not. I bought them from a vendor at the flea market, I showed the receipt to the police."

"I know, but they're his nonetheless. I recognize them. I did the first time I saw them, I just didn't want to believe it. I spoke to the vendor and he told me that one of his regular suppliers, a pothunter, brought them to him. I suspect Morgan's murderer fenced them to him."

She finished her drink in one gulp.

"Oh, God," she said. "That's awful."

"That's not all. Did you hear Denise McGrath has an alibi for the time of Morgan's death?"

"Yeah, I did."

"That Klett's plane was sabotaged? Someone stuffed rags in the fuel tanks."

"No," she said. "I didn't know that." For the first time she seemed to understand the seriousness of what he was trying to say. "I'm glad you're not dead, by the way."

"Thanks."

"Do the police know who did it?"

"Brad Lowery doesn't have an alibi for Morgan's murder, and he was alone at the airport near Klett's plane long enough to sabotage the fuel tanks."

"So he killed Morgan because he knew he'd vote for studying the skeleton, and Klett why?"

"Because he was working on a compromise that would still give scientists access to the skeleton."

"That's that, then."

"I'm not so sure. It's too easy, too obvious. I believe Lowery sabotaged the airplane, but I don't think he killed Morgan."

"I'm not following you. Must be lack of sleep. Are you implying that there are two murderers? One who killed Morgan and one who killed Klett?"

"Exactly."

Simon pulled the arrowhead out of his pocket. "I found this up in the mountain and it gave me an idea," he said.

She took it from him. "It's just an arrowhead."

"What's it made of?"

"Rhyolite, of course."

"But Uwharrie Man's point is flint."

"There's flint in Virginia and South Carolina. It must have come from there."

"There's flint in Saône-et-Loire, in France, too."

Understanding dawned. It was clear in Martha's widening eyes, her open mouth, the way her hand went to her throat.

"Oh, my God! Dr. Mabry spent three summers excavating at the Solutré Cave! He could have stolen that point!"

"Do you think he's capable of it?"

"Yes, yes, I do. But to fake a find like Uwharrie Man? It would be almost impossible."

"I expect that the skeleton and the hearth were genuine. I think he found those on an earlier dig and didn't reveal them, saving the discovery for a more opportune time. You need human bones, something datable through radiocarbon testing, like a charcoal hearth, and cultural evidence, like the point, to make a really important discovery. He had the first two, and got tired of waiting for the third. He salted the find with a Solutrean point he acquired in France."

"He set me up! He sent me to that spot to dig! I was the least experienced person on the team! I'm screwed—everyone will think I was part of it! I'll never work in archaeology again—no one will even let me sift dirt!"

"Unless you help me prove this. If you're part of unmasking Mabry, then your academic reputation will be intact. You could find another thesis advisor. It'll be tough, but it can be done. I'll help you, I know some people."

13

I don't know.

—THE LAST WORDS OF PETER ABELARD, 1079–1142,
THE MOST NOTED PHILOSOPHER OF HIS TIME

SIMON EXPLAINED TO MARTHA, OVER A DELIVERY PIZZA, what he thought had happened. Lawrence Mabry was out on an early morning jog, walking his dog, whatever, just happening to be in Morgan's neighborhood, when he saw Morgan's light on and stopped for a chat. At some point in their conversation Morgan told him he planned to vote to study Uwharrie Man, but that he had questions about the spear point, and he suggested that Mabry should trace it to its quarry despite the expense. He must have had a reason for this, but Simon didn't know what it was, just that Morgan was studying ore provenance that night on the Internet. Mabry had counted on being in complete control of the study, being in charge of making the decisions. When he realized that Morgan's request would reveal where the point originated, he knew he'd be ruined, so he killed him. He sedated the dogs and stole cash and artifacts to make it look like a burglary gone bad. Then he disposed of the murder weapon.

"And then Lowery killed Klett?"

"Klett proposed a compromise that was bound to pass. Lowery would lose the publicity vehicle that was powering his congressional campaign."

"Kind of obvious, isn't it?"

"Yeah, but hard for the police to prove without more evidence. Motive and opportunity won't be enough to prosecute him."

"You said I could help, I could salvage my career?"

"Yes, by telling the police everything you've told me. That Mabry could have acquired a Solutrean point in France, that he had the opportunity to salt the Uwharrie Man dig, that he intentionally sent you to dig in that spot, that in previous years he had plenty of opportunity to find the skeleton, that he didn't intend to have the point analyzed."

"Let's go," she said. "Wait, I look terrible. Let me wash my face and change clothes."

"Sure," Simon said.

Martha went into her bedroom and came out a few minutes later, hair brushed, face washed, wearing a fresh shirt.

Outside the door she paused.

"Forgot my keys," she said. She stepped back into her apartment and came back out, dangling her keys, and locked the door behind her.

"Let's take both cars," she said. "I might need mine later. I'll follow you."

———

S<small>IMON PARKED OUTSIDE THE</small> Museum of Natural Sciences. Martha pulled up behind him and got out of her car.

"Why are we here?" she asked. "Aren't we going to the police station?"

"I want to ask Dr. Klett's secretary a question," Simon said. "If she's here. About his funeral. Won't take a minute."

When they were inside the elevator, Simon mashed the button for the basement.

"Wrong floor," she said.

Simon took her arm. "No, it's not."

"Dr. Mabry's lab is down there! I don't want to see him!"

"Yes, you do."

She lunged at the buttons on the elevator.

"Simon, no! I'm about to turn the man in to the police! I don't want to see him!"

"It's okay, I called him before I went to your apartment. He's expecting us. I want to see if I can pull some more information out of him. I need you to be there so you can tell me later if he's lying or not, be a witness."

"Shouldn't the police do this?"

"Honey, then he'll be on his guard. Right now he doesn't know we suspect him of anything."

When the elevator door opened, Simon led her out into the hall. Once there, she composed herself, and went down the hall with him.

When they got to the lab door, Martha entered her code and the door sprang open. Mabry was at a computer. He looked up at them and nodded.

"Hi, Martha, hello, Simon. You look well, for having survived a plane crash."

Mabry wore another rock star outfit, black jeans and a black polo shirt. His sunglasses were hooked in his collar.

He nodded across the room at a coffee machine. "I've made fresh coffee, and I think there are some cookies over there somewhere."

Simon filled a mug, but Martha didn't. She sat on a metal folding chair, looking a bit pale but otherwise composed.

"I feel so terrible about Dr. Klett, about everything that's happened," Mabry said. "Who knew that Uwharrie Man could arouse such emotions in people? Well, shall we get to work?"

"Dr. Mabry thinks we're here to draft a letter to the governor requesting implementation of Klett's compromise," Simon said to Martha. "At least, that's what I told him when I called."

"Despite the horror of these murders, my responsibility is still to the scientific study of Uwharrie Man," Mabry said. "I'm sure this is what Dr. Morgan and Dr. Klett would have wanted us to do."

"Actually," Simon said, sliding up onto a metal table and pulling out his notebook, "could we settle a few other things first?"

"What?" he asked.

"I just want to get a few points clear in my own head about all this. After all, my best friend was murdered. And I'm supposed to make a statement at police headquarters later today, and I'd like to get the sequence of events clearer in my head."

"Sure," Mabry said. "Anything I can do to help."

"Me, too," Martha said. "Anything."

"First of all," Simon said, making a point of flipping

through his notes, "was Martha Dunn alone when she discovered Uwharrie Man?"

Martha started.

"Why, yes. I scouted the site originally, but I did set her to work on the location," Mabry said.

"Was she alone when she discovered the point?"

Martha picked her purse up off the floor and clutched it to her chest.

"Why, yes," Mabry said. "It was several days later, after the first layers of dirt were brushed away. I thought that since Martha discovered the skeleton, she should have the opportunity to excavate it."

"So she could have planted the point."

Mabry stared at Martha, then at Simon.

"What on earth . . . ," he said.

"Uwharrie Man was the dissertation topic dreams are made of, a ticket straight to an assistant professorship, a book contract, and membership in the faculty club. All the site lacked was a pre-Clovis artifact to corroborate the carbon-14 date. Tell me," Simon said to Martha, "where did you get the point? On eBay?"

Martha jumped to her feet. "What are you doing?" she said to Simon, flushing from her neck to her hairline.

"What's going on?" Mabry said. "What are you implying?"

"I have a critical question for you," Simon said to Mabry, "one that you must answer truthfully, if you don't want to be questioned in both these murders."

Mabry nodded, looking worried.

"When I called Klett to tell him about the contents of Morgan's notes," Simon said, "he told me you were with him in the office."

"That's right."

"What did you do afterwards?"

"Well, he and I discussed the compromise."

"For how long?"

"I'm not sure."

"Then what did you do?"

"I came down here to work."

"Was Martha with you in Klett's office? Sure she was. She carries your briefcase, gets your coffee, basks in your reflected glory. She was there. Did she come down here with you?"

"No," Mabry said, staring at Martha as if she'd sprouted horns. "No. She gave Klett a lift to the airport."

Martha exploded, screaming at them. "I did not!" she said. "I remembered I had to be somewhere! He took a taxi!"

"You're a beautiful woman," Simon said. "The guys at the airport will remember you."

"Okay," she said. "I took him to the airport. I was stupid to deny that. But I didn't sabotage the plane! That was done in Lumberton!"

"I don't think so," Simon said. "I don't think anyone can say how long it took for those rags to block the fuel outlets."

"What are you trying to do to me?" she screamed at him.

Simon leaned his weight on his hands to keep them from shaking.

"The morning Morgan was killed was a Monday. You teach an eight o'clock morning class in introductory prehistory every Monday, Wednesday, and Friday. You told me you usually got up early to go to the waffle house to prepare. Would anyone at the restaurant be able to remember if you were there that Monday?"

"I overslept," she said.

"Don't think so," Simon said. "I think you saw Morgan's light on when you drove by his house and stopped to chat. That's when you learned that he wanted to establish the provenance for the point, a very expensive process, one Mabry didn't think was necessary. When the study proved that the raw flint from which the point was made came from a quarry in Europe, you'd be found out. So you smashed in Morgan's skull with a handy geode, drugged the dogs so the police would think the murderer was a stranger to them, and stole some cash and the artifacts. You fenced the artifacts, but when you saw them on display right here in Raleigh at our own flea market, you panicked and bought them back. Stupid of you to keep them at your apartment."

"Jesus H. Christ," Mabry said, his fists clenched at his side. "You salted the Uwharrie Man dig site! What were you thinking? You've made me look like a fool!"

"It's all about you," Martha said, "always has been. What did I ever have to show for the years I spent doing your grunt work? I hope you have to resign and teach junior college for the rest of your life, then you'll see what my life is like."

"I don't think Dr. Mabry suggested you seduce me so you could search my house. You came up with that plan all by yourself," Simon said. "You needed those notes in case Morgan wrote that the spear point ore should be traced."

"I thought I knew you," Mabry said to her. "How did you learn to be so vicious?"

"Look in the mirror," Martha said.

Mabry picked up his cell phone from his desk and flipped it open.

Martha pulled her handgun out of her purse.

"Don't even think about it," she said to Mabry. "And you," she said to Simon, "Professor Midget, you're not as brilliant as you think you are. I got my gun when I went back into the apartment for my keys. And my passport, too. There's some nylon cord in the supply closet. Tie up Indiana Jones over there, then I'll do the same to you."

"Martha," Simon said, "I took the bullets out of the gun while you were in your bedroom changing."

Mabry flipped open his phone again.

SIMON SAT IN MORGAN's battered recliner for the last time, waiting for the truck from the charity shop to arrive and cart away the furniture. His work was nearly done. The only task left was to supervise the contractor he'd hired to fix up Morgan's house so it would fetch a good price. The Kenan College Library staff had come and crated up all Morgan's books and papers and taken them to the special collections room at the library. Simon gave Morgan's laptop to Trina so she could surf the Internet to her heart's content. He donated the camper to the Office of State Archaeology to use as a mobile office. He kept Morgan's country and bluegrass music collection for himself. Clare Monahan had arrived back in the country several days ago, and they'd spent an emotional evening together at Players' Retreat. Yesterday he'd attended Henry Klett's funeral.

He learned from Otis Gates that Martha Dunn had accepted a plea agreement, one that would allow her to spend the rest of her life in a prison a few states away, near her family. That was a blessing. He wouldn't have to testify at her trial, facing her at the defendant's table, nor would he have to live the rest of his life knowing that she languished in Women's Prison, just a couple of miles from his home. It would be easier to forget her.

Simon was tired of death and dying and of dealing with all the emotions that went along with them. He was overdue for a sabbatical. He would take up Morgan's suggestion. Going down the Nile sounded like an excellent plan to him.